Voice of Vengeance

VOICE OF VENGEANCE

Juanita Tyree Osborne

AVALON BOOKS
THOMAS BOUREGY AND COMPANY, INC.
NEW YORK

PRINTED IN THE UNITED STATES OF AMERICA
BY HADDON CRAFTSMEN, SCRANTON, PENNSYLVANIA

Voice of Vengeance

CHAPTER ONE

On reaching the front door, Meghan heard the phone. She fumbled for her key but, hampered as she was by gloves, packages, and twilight, she could not find it easily. Somewhere in the clutter of her enormous handbag, though, that key was hiding.

Meanwhile, the phone kept ringing through the house. She muttered, fumed, found the key, dropped it, then finally got the door open.

Inside, flinging purse and bundles every which way, she ran for the phone that was tucked away in the bedroom. In the dim light Meghan banged into things and stepped on the cat's tail.

"Sorry, Dido," she said as the cat shrieked.

She was convinced the minute she picked up the phone it would stop ringing, and she would be left to wonder all evening who had called.

But such was not the case, unfortunately.

The person on the other end was persistent. She could say that for him.

Breathlessly, almost frantically, she said, "Hello."

"Meg, is that you?"

"Yes, it is." Tugging off her gloves with her teeth, she tried to place the low, strained, whispery voice. Sounded like someone with a bad case of laryngitis.

There followed a flood of mumbling, a mass of unintelligible words. Like molten lava from an erupting volcano, the stream of garbled words poured over her. Holding the mouthpiece away from her, she stared at it. One more chance you get, she told it silently.

"What—what did you say?" she asked, her free hand batting around for the lamp on the nightstand. Suddenly the darkness of the house was filled with leaping terrors. Light helped but not much. She remained tense, her nerves bunched up.

Silly, she chided herself, the speaker isn't here in the house, after all.

But wherever he was, he began to get through to her with a message of hate. From a soft, hissing tirade he went on to a more vitriolic attack.

Oh, dear, one of those. And to think she had almost broken her neck getting to the phone to listen to such garbage!

She started to hang up. That was what one was supposed to do in such cases, hang up. But something held her. A peculiar awareness was drifting through her, and she had the vague, disturbing notion she knew the person on the other end. A known identity floated around in the murky waves of her subconscious. She felt she had heard this man speak sometime or other.

Only, why did she think it was a man? It could be a woman. The person was obviously disguising her/his voice, but she caught a certain indefinable nuance, a shading in tone, a spacing of words, something that was tantalizingly familiar.

Could she be deliberately blocking out his identity? she wondered. A man again. He—she—whoever knew her well enough to call her by the shortened version of her name, Meg.

She listened more intently, despite the queasy, shrinking sensation below her heart. Who among the people she knew or thought she knew hated her so much? What had she done?

Suddenly a chill went through her as out of the hodgepodge came a distinct, direct threat.

"Kill—I'm going to kill you, Meg Latimer, because you're not fit to live! Prepare yourself. Say your prayers, if you know any. You haven't much time left."

"Who are you?" she asked shrilly, wanting him to speak up.

A laugh, broken and out of control, sounded in her ear, sending fresh shivers over her. "Think I would tell you? You never were very smart, Meg Latimer."

That was all except for some heavy, hate-filled breathing. That, of course, was part of the torture. He wanted her to know he was still there, invisible, unmovable. Hair lifted on the back of her neck. This was worse than verbal assault. Unknown, unseen, he seemed to possess all the advantages, his murderous hostility crackling along the telephone wires.

Again she demanded, "Who are you?"

He went on breathing. Of course, he wasn't going to tell, but she wished he would say something and perhaps give himself away. There was only the loud, ominous breathing, though.

Enough. She banged down the receiver and stood staring at it, as if it were a coiled-up snake. It had the wet imprint of her hand on it. The caller had achieved his or her purpose—scared the living daylights out of her.

Her head swam and her legs shook so hard that she could scarcely stand. Slowly she sank onto the bed and, sitting hunched there, began telling herself this would pass. The shakes, the icy sweat, all of it would fade and she would be her old steady self again.

Thank heaven she was not entirely alone. From the doorway, Dido watched her with glassy amber eyes. She hadn't forgiven Meghan for stepping on her beautiful bushy tail. No doubt she, Meghan, had wounded other creatures, human and otherwise, in her twenty-two years. But she had never meant to—she wasn't cruel. No, she wasn't.

But the caller was. Very cruel. And Meghan knew what she should do, what one was supposed to do when one received a threatening call—notify the police and phone company.

An old obstinate loyalty kept her from doing either. Because it could have been Jon. When very drunk he sounded a little like that. Oh, not vicious but slurred and incoherent. He might have gone back to drinking, even though only that morning he had promised he never would again. Ah, but he had sworn off before.

Still, she could not imagine Jon . . . But then one never knew what he would do while drinking. And as long as there was a chance of it being Jon, she would not call the police. Or if there was a chance of it being another member of the Deverell family.

No, she would rather think it someone else, an unhappy customer or slighted acquaintance. Yet such a person would not have been likely to call her Meg. Well, it might have been a classmate who had borne a grudge all these years. The ill feeling may have smoldered inside the person until finally he or she made the call.

Now that person may have got it out of his/her system. Meghan hoped so, and that was all there was to it. No need getting all upset, going to pieces. Lots of people got these stupid, meaningless calls. It was quite common these days. Too bad such nincompoops didn't have better things to do.

But if it were such a caller, why couldn't

she dismiss it? Because it had been a shock—she hadn't been prepared. She had believed herself to be well-liked. No one would want to upset and alarm her. So she had thought. But it was not true. Someone hated her with a vengeance. It hadn't been the usual nuisance call, the usual kid having a bit of fun.

It had been more of a personal thing. But what had she done to arouse such venom? How had she wronged someone? But then, she needn't be guilty. A person with a twisted, warped mind need only imagine she had wronged him or her.

Oh, that voice! It was trapped inside her skull, not only the spoken words but the viperous hostility behind them. That harangue could have been delivered in Hindustani and she would still have perceived the malevolence. She would have known at once the caller despised her, wanted her dead.

According to him, she had only a short time left. She glanced nervously at the clock ticking away on the bedside table. It was a drained, dismal time of the day—going on six—to have something like this happen. She was tired enough already. Her nerves had been frayed by the day as it was. Now this on top of everything else. Quite enough to floor her.

Still staring at the clock, Meghan realized it was time to prepare the light meal she usually had in the evening. But she certainly wasn't hungry. How could she eat with that slurred, sibilant voice going around in her head? "Kill—I'm going to kill you..."

Abruptly she got up. Better check the windows and doors, make sure they were locked securely. This was the first time she had been afraid since living alone. Now that she thought about it, her 1930 bungalow was on a corner lot and somewhat isolated.

She had only one really close neighbor, an elderly widow. Mrs. Macklin had a big dog, though, who would probably raise a ruckus were she to scream out. And then Mrs. Macklin would come to her rescue. When she wore her hearing aid, Mrs. Macklin could hear as well as anyone and she kept knives, hatchets, cans of pepper, and a loaded pistol within easy reach.

Meghan thought she might do well to do the same, for her home was also her place of business. She had converted one end of the house into a shop after Aunt Duffy died. The old woman had left it all to her—the house, furniture, belongings, a bit of money, and Dido, her beloved cat.

Her attic, Meghan discovered, was heaped with odd pieces of furniture, old clocks, brass pieces, barrels of old glass and china, trunks of clothing, and heaps of magazines and books, as well as other items. Enough of that sort of thing to open a small trash-and-treasure shop, which Meghan had promptly done. She made enough to buy groceries and more trash and treasure. Mostly trash.

That unsettling November evening, walk-

ing through her house and shop, Meghan
wished she had taken Mrs. Macklin's advice
and bought a dog—a killer dog. But she hadn't
wanted to put Dido through that. Dido was
old and set in her ways. A dog of any kind
could very well finish her off, and then Aunt
Duffy would turn over in her grave.

But Dido or no Dido, Meghan just might
have to get a dog. Provided, of course, she did
not go back to Jon, marry him, and live on the
Deverell plantation, Blackthorn. But that
would not be for a while, anyway. This time
they were having a "trial engagement." If at
the end of six months he was still dry, they
would marry. Oh, how she was keeping her
fingers crossed!

After checking and double-checking all windows and doors, Meghan went into the tiny,
red-checked kitchen and turned on the flame
under the teakettle. Then she gave Dido something to eat. Her hands were still shaking and
she felt slightly nauseated. Better not try to
eat herself just yet. But a good bracing cup of
tea might help.

While waiting for the pot to boil, she continued to tear her brain apart. Who had called
her? Who of all the people she knew? One of
the many faces swimming before her had made
that call.

Yes, yes, she knew it was the duty of the
police to find the one responsible, but probably
the first person they would want to question
would be Jon, then other members of his fam-

ily. Like most families, the Deverells had some weird ones.

With her steaming cup, Meghan sat down at the breakfast table and began in earnest to sort through her memory for some clue. So engrossed was she, she put three heaping spoons of sugar in her tea before she noticed what she was doing.

Dido came over, rubbed against her legs, and curled up on her icy feet. The cat wasn't much protection, Meghan knew, but she felt better with Dido's purring presence.

Still, her thoughts kept circling back to the phone call. She was on the verge of delving deep into her past when she stopped herself. True, the animosity could be long-standing, but what had she done recently to touch it off? It had to be bad enough to make someone want to kill her.

Going to the cupboard, Meghan took two aspirins and washed them down with the icky-sticky tea. Then she resumed her pondering. She seemed stuck with two conclusions:

(1) It was someone she had known in the past.

(2) And wronged recently.

Recently. Why not start with today? Pouring herself another cup of tea, Meghan began reviewing the day leading up to her wild dash to the phone.

CHAPTER TWO

The gray Monday that had ended with the terrifying phone call had started with a different kind of excitement. Ordinarily Meghan closed her shop on Mondays and went out looking for salable items, haunting estate sales, junk stores, garage sales, old farmhouses, auctions, and flea markets.

Not so this morning. Around nine she had headed the station wagon out toward the Deverell plantation, Blackthorn. Blackthorn. The very name had a romantic appeal, but she was determined not to be swayed by that. She had to make a serious decision.

The day before, after a quiet Sunday-afternoon date, she and Harley Felton had decided to be married. That is, they had almost decided. First she had to see Jon, to make sure there was nothing left of her feeling for him. It would not be fair to Harley to marry him while she was still in love with Jon.

11

And Meghan had another secret reason for seeing Jon, one she was loath to admit even to herself. She wanted to see if he had finally pulled himself together and stopped drinking.

Although Harley saw him every day, he never mentioned Jon, and Meghan could never bring herself to inquire about him, but she was curious. It really wouldn't make any difference whether he had quit drinking or not. She planned to go ahead and marry Harley. It was just that she still cared enough to be concerned about Jon. After all, they had been very close, shared much together.

She hoped he had got straightened out and would be sober when she reached Blackthorn. He should be at ten in the morning. Then they could have a friendly little talk. She was fairly sure he would be reasonable about her intention to marry Harley. Jon had never blamed her for backing out on their wedding day.

"Frankly, Meg, I don't see how you've put up with me this long," he had said at their last meeting.

Since then she had not set foot on Deverell soil and had no idea what had become of him. She was afraid to think...

She had made a clean break. She had gone to Memphis, and Aunt Duffy had taken her in.

"It's what I should have done when your poor mother died instead of letting you go live with them wild Deverells," Aunt Duffy said, her old, sallow face puckered with regret.

"But I thought I was too old to be raising you, and I figured they could give you the advantages I couldn't. Now look at you, all broken-hearted over the young scamp."

Aunt Duffy was never one for propping up another's drooping spirits. She left that up to the one whose spirits drooped. And Meghan had pulled herself out of the depths. More than that, she had learned to do and to think for herself, something she had not done at Blackthorn. There she had leaned on others, depended on them to think and do for her.

Getting back to the morning just behind her, she had not dressed up for Jon. She had deliberately worn her usual treasure-hunting outfit—scarf around her head, chamois jacket, unpressed slacks, well-worn boots. She would be casual about the visit. This was something she should do. It was not a romantic rendezvous. Besides, it was starting to drizzle.

And yet she could not really be casual about Jon Mark Deverell. No need kidding herself about that. It made no difference that she had grown up with him and should be used to him. She knew a certain excitement merely thinking about him. But that could be only a lingering of the old infatuation, nothing more. Anyway, she was going to find out.

Truly, her feelings about Harley—warm, reliable Harley—were different from the feelings she'd had for Jon. And perhaps for that very reason she and Harley could have a better chance of making a go of it. Their affection seemed more real, more mature—so different from the head-swirling, soul-searing emotion she'd felt for Jon.

After all, she was no longer the mindless, head-over-heels-in-love girl she had been. That trembling, desperate bride waiting at the church was gone. Now she was free—free to make a wise decision, to marry a steady, reliable, lovable man, to have a family and a peaceful home. She could never have had that with Jon, at least not with him drinking.

And, of course, Meghan did love Harley Felton and always had. She'd respected him greatly, turned to him in time of trouble, confided in him, and he had always been there, solid as a rock—and sober.

"Everything my son is not, that's Harley," Edward Deverell had once remarked, especially for Jon's benefit. "If only you would assume your responsibilities, my boy, I would not have to hire an outsider to help around here."

Jon had merely shrugged and turned away with that go-to-the-devil smile of his, while Harley had gone from hired hand to farm manager, ever rising in Edward Deverell's estimation.

Yes, Meghan felt marriage with Harley Felton would work where it would have failed miserably with Jon. Of course, it meant Harley would have to give up his job at Blackthorn and the charming little house by the lake. But he had saved enough to make a down payment on a farm of his own. It was time he, too, cut himself away from the Deverells. She did not need them and Harley did not need them.

Since the plantation was about fifty miles out of Memphis, Meghan had time to think on the drive. And memory, like a magic carpet, carried her back to that long-ago time when she had first gone to Blackthorn.

She had been nine, red-elbowed, pigtailed, skinny, homeless—the proverbial poor relative. But Jon's mother, Katherine Deverell, had welcomed her with open arms.

"Your dear mother and my stepfather were distant cousins, but you will be more than cousin here, my child. I've always wanted a daughter."

So, although Meghan was not even a blood relative, she had become the daughter of the house and almost as pampered as Jon, the only son. They hadn't been alike, though. He was daring, full of mischief, while she was on the shy side, quieter.

All the same, she adored him from the beginning. He was five years older and darkly handsome, although slightly scarred on one side of his face.

"Fell out of the top of that tree there," he said, pointing to the tallest oak in the yard. "Haven't been the same since. That scar is a symbol of my flawed personality."

A sign of his reckless nature, Meghan was more inclined to believe. He probably climbed that tree because his father had told him not to. He was always rebelling against his father. The two of them did not get along well at all, and it was something of a blessing the old man did not live to see his only son take to drink. Then again, if Edward Deverell hadn't died and in the manner he did, Jon might not have turned to alcohol.

"I never made him proud," Jon said once in drunken remorse. "He always thought more of Harley—wanted me to be like Harley—but I'm not Harley. I'm me, Jon Mark Deverell."

On through the drizzling morning, Meghan drove, handling the station wagon with the dexterity she had acquired in the months of owning it. It had been necessary in hauling stuff around for the shop.

She was rather glad she wasn't out scouting for relics in that wet weather, wading through mud, getting stuck in a farmhouse drive, poking around some drafty barn or dusty attic. Usually, she found her treasure-hunting interesting. What joy there was in finding an old kerosene lamp, an uncracked churn, a piece of Depression glass, or a first edition.

But on this particular day—the day that was to end with the awful phone call—she had other matters on her mind. No, not other matters—a person. Somberly tall, elegantly indolent, an ironic smile on his scarred, aristocratic face, he dominated everything else flitting around in her head.

Meghan drove through the Tennessee landscape, scarcely seeing it. The thin gray rain obscured most of it, anyway. She caught mere glimpses of farmhouses, wide fields, and stretches of woods. She only knew she was getting closer to Deverell country—where he was.

And so it had been since that long-ago day when first she had arrived at Blackthorn and fallen under Jon's spell.

Oh, there had been the others—motherly Cousin Katherine, her husband, Edward, and his stepbrother, Roland, and Roland's wife, Zena, and their children, Stephanie and Terrence. Then there had been Flory Atkins, the cook, Simonds, the yardman, and eventually Harley.

But all of them faded into the background when Jon was around. She saw only him and, although tormented by his occasional drinking after his parents died, she had agreed to marry him. But he had not given up the bottle. Right up to the day they were to have been married, he continued to drink heavily on occasion. Too heavily. She and her love had not been able to blot out whatever he wished to escape from. Only in drinking could he hide, and she suspected he wasn't truly able to hide there.

When he had finally shown up for their wedding, he was roaring drunk, and Meghan knew it was no use. She couldn't go through with it. Her veil flying, she had dashed from the church. Packing up, crying buckets, she had shaken the dust of Blackthorn from her heels.

Jon had not tried to stop her, had not come after her. She wondered if he were relieved. Now he could drink in peace without her nagging.

Thinking on all this, Meghan was more than a little depressed by the time she reached the plantation. The wrought-iron gates stood open and probably had done so since the ruinous night Jon had tried to drive through one of them.

Maneuvering the station wagon between the stone pillars, she started up the wet, pebbly drive. Through the fine rain she saw the dark tracery of leafless trees and the imposing outline of the house on the slope rising before her. Massive with gables, turrets, and soaring chimneys, it towered against the dreary sky.

She gazed at it with aching throat and misting eyes. After all that had happened, after all this time, it was still home, the not-to-be-denied residence of her heart. What carefree children she and Jon had been playing on those wide, rolling lawns. Then they began to grow up, and their hearts had grown even closer. They could have been so happy, if only . . .

But there was no need to go into all that. Meghan just hoped he was sober today. But then, what if he had quit drinking altogether? Her heart beat a little faster at the hope. Still, she mustn't go building up her hopes only to have them come crashing down. She wasn't coming here to be reconciled with Jon.

It was all like a dream, anyway—the Victorian mansion shrouded in misting rain with veiled woods and river off to one side and the lake and Harley's cottage to the other.

Reminded of Harley, Meghan felt a pang of guilt. He hadn't wanted her to come to Blackthorn and confront Jon for the last time.

"Why put yourself through that? There's no need for it." His rugged, square-jawed face had been shaded with accusation and in his deepset eyes there had been a subtle dread. He had been afraid Jon would hypnotize her, as he always had, and she would go back to him.

"But, Harley, I have to know my feelings for sure!"

He had reached across the table, pressed her hand. "I know, Meghan, I know. But I just don't like seeing you take the chance of getting hurt again, and I don't want to lose you, not that I ever had you the way he did."

No one would ever have her love again the way Jon had. But then that had been infatuation. Love was the mature kind of feeling she shared with Harley.

As Meghan approached the sprawling house, she braced herself, fought against the sinking feeling, doubts, and shyness that had left her vulnerable in the past. Now she must hold her own, be calm and sensible, as she had learned to be these last two years.

But how unnerving it was, coming back! Unreal. She could scarcely believe she had ever lived in that old haze-bound house. And the Deverells themselves were like ghostly characters moving through the shadows of her imagination.

The actual and true was what she had found since leaving Blackthorn, and that was what she had to hold on to. She must not lose herself in this old, insubstantial world. Not again.

CHAPTER THREE

Rattling by the camellia shrubs massed against the side of the house, Meghan parked in the back under a big dripping willow that now had only a few brown leaves.

Filled with a strange mixture of dread and delight, she stepped out of the station wagon, her feet sinking into the soggy ground. It seemed hardly more solid than the vaporous air swimming around her. As insidious and ready to swallow her up as quicksand, she thought as she started toward the well-remembered back steps.

Well-remembered, too, were the ghostly out-buildings and farther away the red tin-roofed barn that Flory had said had vampire bats.

"If they fly in your hair, you'll go crazy," she had warned, thereby keeping Meghan a safe distance from the barn.

Meghan had almost reached the steps when

she saw old Simonds turning the corner of the
house. She heard herself laugh. She was even
glad to see the grouchy yardman. And he was
wearing the same mackinaw and cap with the
lappets over his ears. His face with the long
thin jaws and hollow cheeks wore its usual
scowl. That did not necessarily mean he did
not recognize her, wasn't glad to see her. It
was simply his normal look.

"Simonds, Simonds," she said, going to him
and shaking his cold, rough hands. "Don't you
remember me, Meghan?"

"So you've come back," he said after a moment, his close-set eyes fixed on her, his mouth
thin and unsmiling.

"Well, not really, Simonds. I've only come to
see Mr. Jon. Is he inside?"

"Can't say, miss. More'n likely he's gone for
his morning ride."

"Morning ride?" Meghan stared at the old
man. That sounded like the old Jon, the Jon
who did not drink.

"Yes, miss, he rides every day now, rain or
shine," said Simonds, not without pride. If he
had ever cared about anyone, it had been Jon.
But then Jon could charm the birds off the
trees.

"Oh, Simonds, then he's not—?" She was
almost afraid to hope.

He shook his head. "Mr. Jon ain't touched
a drop in nearly two years now."

"How wonderful. I'm so pleased," she said.
Only, pleased wasn't the word. A new heaven

and earth were opening up. Jon wasn't drinking, thank God, thank God.

Meghan became conscious of Simonds watching her narrowly, not saying anything. She wondered if the old fellow blamed her for Jon's drinking. Jon hadn't stopped until she left. Was Simonds afraid she would stay and Jon would start all over again?

"Well, I'll be inside—for a while anyway," Meghan said awkwardly. "If you see Mr. Jon, please tell him I'm here."

He touched his cap and hobbled off, muttering darkly to himself. She mustn't pay any attention to him. He was always a surly, unpleasant man.

Anyway, she was too filled with the good news to think about anything else. Jon wasn't drinking, that was all that mattered. Was it possible? If so, why hadn't Harley told her? He lived on the grounds and saw Jon every day—he must have known. But then she and Harley were always careful not to discuss Jon.

Never mind Harley. Jon wasn't drinking and she was home, and breathing the wet, pungent scent of the cedars pressing against the kitchen windows, breathing the damp, almost living scent of the old house itself, the familiar none-like-it smell of home. And Jon wasn't drinking!

Impatiently wiping the weak ecstatic tears from her eyes, Meghan glanced up to see a curtain fall back in place. She felt a prickling at the nape of her neck. Someone had watched her arrival and was probably still watching her from behind the lace curtain upstairs. She could almost see his or her shadow. It bothered her, made her feel uneasy, having those furtive eyes on her. She was no stranger. The person up there could have opened the window and waved to her, called down to her, welcomed her.

So far Meghan wasn't being warmly received. Simonds certainly hadn't been overjoyed to see her, but then that contrary old man wouldn't have shown it if he had been. No matter, no matter, Jon wasn't drinking. Like a song it ran through her head: Jon wasn't drinking, wasn't drinking.

Running up the weathered steps, as she had so many times in the past, Meghan started to open the door, then hesitated. She didn't live here anymore. She had better knock. Her heart and knees were knocking, too. But how strange to be knocking at this dearly loved house.

She heard Flory exclaim in the kitchen, "Who on earth—?"

This was followed by cautious, suspicious footsteps and a cautious, suspicious opening of the door. They didn't open up to just anyone at Blackthorn.

Seeing who it was, Flory flung the door wide. "Why, why, Miss Meghan!" With her old absentminded smile, she pulled Meghan inside.

She hadn't changed much, thought Meghan. She looked very much as she had when Meghan first met her. She was in her late fifties now, but her chestnut hair was only slightly frosted, her figure still trim. Her pale, pretty face was delicately lined, her hazel eyes turned toward each other, as if looking inward at herself. Whatever she saw seemed to confuse her. She always seemed a bit ill at ease.

Meghan felt ill at ease herself, not quite herself. She did not know why this should be. She had lived in this house much of her life and should not feel uncomfortable here.

"Let me have your coat, Miss Meghan," said Flory. "My, I know Mr. Jon will be glad to see you. He went out riding, but I expect he'll be back directly."

"Yes, I want to see him," said Meghan, deciding to wait here in the kitchen for him. He would probably be coming through the back door. Her heart leaped in anticipation. How would he be—not drinking at all?

She propped herself on the tall, red-painted kitchen stool as if she were still a child waiting for Flory's cookies to come out of the oven. A cinnamon aroma was even now filling the kitchen. Spice cake?

"I'll put the coffeepot on and we'll have a cup," said Flory.

"How is everyone, Flory?" asked Meghan.

"Oh, about the same, miss." Her back to Meghan, as she attended to something on the stove, she added, "You heard about Mr. Roland?"

"Yes, Flory, I was sorry to hear about that. Sudden, wasn't it?"

"What? Oh, Mr. Roland. Yes, it was sudden. He was up and well one day and gone the next. His heart."

"I always liked Uncle Roland," said Meghan. He hadn't been her uncle, but he was Jon's stepuncle and had been like an uncle to her. A quiet man, he hadn't been quick-tempered, authoritative, like his stepbrother, Edward. They weren't at all related by blood, which could account for the differences in their personalities. Roland had been dominated by Edward, as well as by his bossy wife, Zena.

Meghan shook her head sadly. "It's hard to believe both Roland and Edward Deverell are gone."

Flory sighed deeply and Meghan saw her as a sad, lonely figure. There hadn't been anything improper between Flory and Edward, but it was no secret she had adored him for years. Once Meghan had seen Edward put an arm across her shoulder in a careless, friendly way and the girl hadn't known any better than to tell Katherine. What a row there had been then and everyone in the house had been angry with Meghan, even Jon.

"But I didn't know," she had sobbed. "I didn't think Mama Katherine would be mad because he liked Flory."

"You don't understand. Father wasn't supposed to be hanging around Flory," Jon explained.

It had all cleared up, or seemed to, and Flory had been allowed to stay on. There really hadn't been anything to the incident, but Flory had gone on adoring "Mr. Edward."

Now she handed Meghan a blue willow cup steaming with rich dark coffee. Meghan sipped appreciatively, wondering if she had really tasted anything since leaving this kitchen.

"What about Aunt Zena and Stephanie and Terrence?" she asked.

"Oh, they—they're about the same," said Flory.

"Too bad," said Meghan, and they both laughed.

Then Flory changed the subject. "You know about Mr. Jon?"

"That he's quit drinking? Yes, Simonds told me and it's just about the best news I ever heard. How is he, Flory? How is he . . . without it?"

"More like he was before he started, Miss Meghan, except now he's grown up and so like . . . "

She broke off and looked away, but not before Meghan saw the gleam of memory in her inward-turned eyes. For Flory the father lived on in his son.

"Oh, Miss Meghan, do you think now he's not drinking at all that you and he might get back together?"

"I don't know, Flory. It may be too late for that, but I do want to see him."

Silently then they drank their coffee and Meghan let her thoughts drift. How different it might have been if Edward Deverell hadn't shot himself.

"It was an accident," said Jon, who had found

his father slumped over in the library. "He was cleaning his guns and..."

An old story but new for them and devastating for Jon. That was when the occasional heavy drinking had started, with his father's death.

"Meg, Meg, if only I hadn't let him down, been what he wanted me to be."

Guilt had fastened on Jon like a second skin, too often driving him to the cut-glass decanter on the sideboard in the dining room. And when his mother had removed the decanter, he had simply found other means of obtaining liquor.

Still, he might have stopped altogether if Katherine hadn't passed away. She was never the same after Edward's sudden death. Not a physically strong woman, she seemed to give up after losing her husband. In six months, she too was gone, and Jon again blamed himself.

"If I'd been any kind of son—someone she could have counted on..."

As his anguished words echoed through her, Meghan heard the kitchen door open behind her.

CHAPTER FOUR

With the old intense feelings rushing through her, Meghan turned expectantly, but it was not Jon coming through the door.

"Zena," she said, trying to smile and not lose confidence in front of this redoubtable woman who had married Roland Deverell, Jon's step-uncle.

But Zena Deverell appeared as imposing as ever and Meghan felt herself turning into the shy young girl who had ducked her head in the presence of this formidable personage with the hard, overly made-up eyes. She did not return Meghan's weak attempt at a smile as she came forward, her fuchsia caftan swishing about her.

"Meghan, so you've come back," she said brusquely, breathing audibly through her flaring nostrils.

At least she's no hypocrite, thought Meghan.

29

Zena was no happier to see her than old Simonds had been. It followed. Meghan posed a threat to Zena's position at Blackthorn. She managed the house now, but if Meghan were to return and marry Jon, that would change.

Then there was the matter of Zena's darlings—Stephanie and Terrence. They could lose whatever chance they had of inheriting Blackthorn if Meghan and Jon married and had children.

"Yes, I would like to see Jon," said Meghan, lifting her head, striving to hold on to the poise she had acquired since being out on her own.

"I can imagine," Zena murmured, sinking into one of the creaking kitchen chairs and reaching for a cigarette.

"I was sorry to hear about Uncle Roland," said Meghan, being sincere about that. She wondered why nice men like him often married horrid women like Zena.

Zena shrugged her plump shoulders, looking not at all like a bereaved widow. She had ruled poor Roland with an iron hand and had tried to rule everyone at Blackthorn.

"She would like to run me," Jon said once. "But I'll not let her—or Father either. I intend doing as I please."

"Are Stephanie and Terrence still at home?" asked Meghan, knowing they were. Harley had told her, but asking about Zena's children might be a way of breaking the ice with her.

Zena nodded, inhaling deeply and watching Meghan with narrowed eyes. Her children, although grown now, were in Meghan's opinion rather spineless and not apt to leave Mama.

"Does Terrence still plan to study law?" inquired Meghan, more to make conversation than anything.

"I think now he plans to follow in his Cousin Jon's footsteps and be a plain old farmer." She threw Meghan a smile as false as the eyelashes she wore. "Speaking of Jon, do you know that, since you left, he's quit drinking?"

This was indeed a low blow, but Meghan answered politely, "Yes, Flory was telling me. I think it's wonderful." Pure joy filled her at the knowledge.

"Yes, thank heaven, Jon has finally settled down and assumed the responsibility of running the plantation, and about time I would say. For years everything was left up to Roland and Harley. No doubt the strain and hard work had a lot to do with poor Roland's death."

She sighed and waved her jeweled hand. "But that is all over and done with now, and Jon has pulled himself together and taken over. Of course, we still have Harley and Simonds to help—and Terrence does his part. We all keep busy here. As you know, Blackthorn's a big place."

Meghan agreed it was. Blackthorn consisted of several thousand acres, and Jon could be anywhere on that vast stretch. No telling what far corner—in the woods, down in the swamp along the river, up on the hazy blue ridge.

Oh, she wished she were with him as in those days gone by—or that he would come inside. She wanted so to see this clear-headed, responsible Jon. It was what she had always hoped and prayed for—his being strong with both feet on the ground. That was what he was meant to be.

Even as she thought this, the door opened and her head spun around, but it was not the one her heart clamored to see.

His young stepcousin, Terrence, ambled in, yawning and disheveled, as if he had just got up. And he planned to be a farmer! He would never make one, getting up at eleven o'clock in the morning. Tall, reedy, he was close to twenty now, only a few years younger than Meghan, but she felt much older. He peered at her with still-drowsy eyes.

She laughed. "Yes, Terrence, it's me, Meghan."

She held out her hand, which he took in a limp, halfhearted way.

"Welcome back. Hey, Flory, got any coffee there to wake me up?"

"Yes, Mr. Terrence, I believe there's a little left over here from breakfast," said Flory, reaching for the pot on the back of the stove. "I'll just warm it up for you."

Terrence flung himself down in the nearest chair and turned lazily to Meghan. "And what brings you to our part of the world, as if I didn't know."

"I wanted to see Jon about something," she said, her face warming.

He grinned, seeing the blush. "I'll just bet. Think you and old Jon might get back together now he's quit the booze?"

"That's not what I've come to see him about," said Meghan, not sure she was telling the truth. In her heart of hearts, wasn't that what she wanted more than anything on this earth?

"Well, whatcha been up to in old Memphis town?" he asked.

"I have a small trash-and-treasure shop," she said.

Sitting in her cloud of smoke, Zena laughed. "Is that a polite way of saying junk store?"

"No, it isn't," said Meghan evenly. "I have some really nice pieces as well as—some not so nice."

"Like living in town?" asked Terrence.

"Yes, but I miss the country."

"I'll bet," said Zena, her expression smug and knowing.

"I don't know, it gets awful quiet around here sometimes," said Terrence. "Especially now that Jon's on the wagon."

"Well, let's just hope he stays on the wagon," said Zena. "Stephanie has been a great help to him—stood by him through it all."

A pang of jealousy running through her, Meghan glanced at Zena quickly. Had Stephanie and Jon become close? Although their fathers had been stepbrothers, they had never seemed particularly interested in each other. As a matter of fact, Meghan had always thought Stephanie had a crush on Harley. But now had she turned to Jon and been a help to him? Or was Zena merely trying to press her daughter toward Jon? He had more to offer than Harley... and they were not blood relatives.

"So how's business?" asked Terrence, accepting the coffee Flory handed him.

"Fine," said Meghan. Actually, she only made enough to get by on, but she was supporting herself. So let these two sneer at her "junk store."

"Got any old guns?" asked Terrence.

With men it was quite often guns, pocket knives, watches, and clocks. Not always, though. Now and then some big six-footer would come in and want to know if she had a butter dish in pink Depression glass with a cabbage-rose design. But the ones Meghan liked best to wait on were those with a penchant for rare books. Quietly they would thumb through the yellowing volumes, communicating with the deathless.

Terrence had inquired about guns, though, and Meghan shook her head.

"No, but I did have a Civil War sword once. Sold it right off the bat, too. But mostly I deal in glassware, china, knickknacks, brass, odd pieces of furniture, and stuff like that."

"The attic here should yield a lot of that," he said with a snort.

"Well, I didn't come here to look for that," said Meghan. But it wasn't a bad idea.

"No?" murmured Zena, studying her intently while her silently asked question hung on the air: "Why did you come?"

And, despite his slouching pose, Terrence watched her too, his sandy-lashed eyes slits of interest. Both he and his mother wanted to know what she was doing here, but Meghan refused to satisfy their curiosity. This was something that concerned her and Jon and Harley.

In the waiting stillness of the kitchen, the back door opened and Jon walked in.

CHAPTER FIVE

Immobolized, Meghan made not a move toward Jon. She could not. And yet at the same time everything inside her rushed toward him. All her agonizing love went out to him, stronger than ever.

For this was the Jon she had hoped and prayed for. Never had he stood so tall, never had he been more charmingly himself, towering there in the doorway. His high cheekbones gleaming with rain, his dark damp hair falling over his forehead, his face shadowy and scarred, he smiled slowly and triumphantly at finding her back in the old country kitchen.

It wasn't the disdainful smile that mocked her for loving him—a drunk. His smile was that of a man who thought himself worthy of being loved, a man who was free to love.

"Meg," he said, taking one giant step toward her but then stopping abruptly.

37

Reading her, as he was always able to do, he must have seen in her pale, staring face that she wasn't quite ready to fly into his arms. He wasn't a mind reader and could not possibly know she had come up here to tell him she was thinking of marrying someone else. But he must have perceived for all her love she had a decision to make—whether to continue her future without him, or perhaps return to him. That was what kept her frozen where she was, her eyes unblinking on him, her lips parted but silent.

Then, too, he knew of her shyness. They were not alone. Flory and Zena and Terrence were looking on as if they were absorbed in a play, watching a scene in which two sweethearts were being reunited after being separated two years.

"Say, Meg, what an unexpected pleasure this is," Jon said with more restraint, not moving toward her and yet expressing his delight in his words. "And how great you're looking—more beautiful than ever."

No one had ever said she was beautiful except Jon. She was not plain, but her face and figure were by no means perfect. She could pass unnoticed in any crowd, and Harley had praised her character. Only to Jon was she beautiful. Jon, who loved her striking auburn hair and blue eyes.

"You're looking great yourself," she said. Never better. But they had to talk, be alone and work things out one way or the other. She made a funny little coughing sound and straightened her shoulders. "Jon, there's something I have to talk to you about."

"There's a fire in the library. At least there was a while ago. You can go in there," Flory suggested.

As Meghan left the kitchen with Jon, she felt Zena and Terrence staring after her, their eyes burning holes in her back. They were not pleased she was here. Indeed, they were not. She sensed their intense displeasure and hostility.

In the deep, drafty hall, Jon, who hadn't taken his dark, glowing eyes off her, said wonderingly, "I can't believe you're back, Meg. I never thought you would want to come back — after what happened. Darling, darling, I'm so sorry about that. I ruined what should have been the best, most important day of our lives. I threw it all away. How could I? I'll never forget you standing there in the sanctuary — all in white, your veil falling about your lovely face, the tears in those sweet, angelic eyes . . ."

"It was a bad time," Meghan said, wanting to cry at the memory of the heartache and torment she had known then. "But I understand you — you have stopped drinking now."

"For the moment I'm not drinking, Meg," he said quietly, honestly, as if unable to promise more than that.

"But Flory said you hadn't —"

"Not since that awful day you left," he said, his face etched with the painful memory. "I hit bottom then, as the expression goes. There was no place for me to go then but to start back up. I got help, which I'm still getting, by the way, and I'm taking it a day at a time."

"I'm so glad, Jon, so glad," she said, close to tears with the joy of it. "You'll be all right now. I know you will."

"You believed in me when no one else did," he said, smiling down at her tenderly, knowing her as no one else did.

Then he opened the door and they went into the library, a room Meghan had ambivalent feelings about. She had happy memories of playing Scrabble there with Jon and of curling up with a good book on a winter night, but it was also the room where Edward Deverell had accidentally shot himself. And that was the beginning of all her and Jon's trouble, when he had started drinking.

She had no way of knowing whether he was thinking about that as he went over and threw another log on the dying fire. Then they huddled near it, watching the flames catch and leap up the chimney. She thought the kindled fire symbolized their love that wasn't dead, after all, never had been. It was burning more brightly than ever.

Inevitably they turned to each other and, with a deep-felt, almost despairing cry, he caught her to him, holding her fiercely as if he never meant to let her go again.

"Meg, Meg, I never stopped loving you, not for one minute. In all the sickness and confusion, you were somehow with me, your lovely face shining through."

He lowered his flawed, firelit face to kiss her, but she held back, feeling there were things to be settled, words to be said before they were emotionally drawn together. They shouldn't rush it this time. They must proceed more slowly, be sure. And there was something she had to tell him—and how she dreaded that!

An eyebrow lifted quizzically, Jon looked at her. "You do still love me, don't you? I'm not mistaken about that?"

"No, I still love you, but—"

It was enough for him that she still loved him and his lips came crashing down on hers. There was no way then she could escape the ardent power of him, no way to escape the love thundering in their hearts. She made some feeble attempt to draw back, but he only drew her closer and pressed his lips more insistently, more forcefully, to hers.

And, as the old rapture seized her, she knew she could never leave him again. She could not run from the love that was so much a part of them, that was enveloping them, binding them together.

But the ecstatic moment could not last forever and they fell slightly away from each other and, looking into his face, she knew she had to tell him. There could be nothing but truth between them.

"Jon, there's something I have to tell you,"

she said. But on seeing his eyes blazing with love, she did not see how she could do it. "I came up here to see...how I felt."

"How you felt?" he said. "Good heavens, Meg, you mean you didn't know...that you doubted for one minute...?"

"Jon, Jon, listen, you're like part of me, but I didn't know that you had stopped drinking, and I knew we couldn't go on as before. I hoped you had changed, but—"

"It was almost too much to hope for?" he said with a touch of the old irony.

"I had no way of knowing," she said. "And, Jon, there's something else I have to tell you."

He merely looked at her and waited.

"You see, when I left here, I was determined to make a new life for myself. I opened the shop, but it wasn't enough. I was lonely and I—I began seeing Harley."

"Harley?" he repeated, staring at her in amazement, his arms falling away from her.

"You must know I was always fond of him. And I wanted a home and family."

"What the devil are you saying?" he asked, his face dark and incredulous. "That you and Harley—that you've married Harley?"

"No, no," she cried, realizing she was going about this all wrong. But better that he know now than find out later. How terrible he looked, though. "He asked me to marry him. He asked me yesterday, and I sort of agreed, but I—I had to come up here first to see how I really felt..."

He pulled her back to him roughly and possessively, saying harshly, "How could you think for one minute there could ever be anyone else for either of us?"

"I didn't, not really," she said. "But, Jon, I couldn't quite forget what happened before—and I knew I couldn't go through that again."

"I know, I know, my darling, that would be hard to forget—my ruining what should have been the sweetest day of our lives," he said, his face clouded with remorse. "And I wish, Meg, I could say it will never happen again, but—"

"What we need is a little more time," she said.

He did not disagree. "Like how much more time?"

"Oh, say six months," she said.

"Six months—that seems like a helluva long time," he said.

"But by then we should be stronger."

"We? It's not your problem, sweetheart."

"I have my own problems, Jon," she said.

He shook his head. "You're the acme of perfection."

"No, you mustn't think that," she said. "I didn't realize how dependent, how timid, how indecisive I was until I went away. I'm still working on my weaknesses."

"For my part, it will not be a sure thing, but I'll say this, my darling, I'll do my darnedest."

"I know you will," she said firmly, believing him as never before.

He kissed her again and again until her

knees shook and her head spun.

"I—I think I had better go," she said when she could, backing away dizzily, the old shyness returning. The drinking Jon had not been so ardent, so demanding.

"You're not staying for lunch?" he asked disappointedly.

"No, there's something I have to do, and the sooner I attend to it, the better," she said, her eyes clouding at the thought of the unpleasant duty before her.

"You have to tell Harley," Jon said, frowning.

She nodded. "Yes, he's coming to town this afternoon to see what I've decided. Oh, Jon, what a fool I was to let him think I could ever marry him! He's the most wonderful friend in the world, but he could never replace you."

"That Harley," he said, shaking his head. "Sneaking in to see you and not saying anything. I often wondered where he was going, who he was going to see. I knew he was seeing someone in Memphis. He always wore a suit and tie. It will be a blow to him, I'm sure, when you tell him about us."

"Yes, I feel so bad about it, I want to tell him right away I can't marry him. It would be unfair to him if I went on letting him think he had a chance."

"I can't say I have too much sympathy for him," Jon said. "Harley should have known we still loved each other, that it would never be over for us."

His arm around her, they moved into the hall. He pressed his lean, scarred cheek against hers. "You want me to court you, Meg, these next six months, woo you all over again with flowers and candy?"

"Anyone would like that," she said, warmed at the thought.

"And you'll stay in that little house of yours in town?" he asked as they walked slowly back toward the kitchen to pick up her coat.

"I think it wise," she said, remembering the feverish kisses in the library.

They were turning into the kitchen when they were stopped by footsteps clattering down the service stairs.

"Meghan Latimer, is that you? Don't tell me you were running off without so much as a hello to your Cousin Stephanie."

CHAPTER SIX

Meghan had never felt particularly close to the scatterbrained Stephanie. But now they embraced and cheek-kissed. Meghan couldn't help remembering what Zena had said about Jon and Stephanie becoming close.

Meghan found this hard to believe. Jon had so little in common with this flighty butterfly. Meghan had to admit, though, Stephanie was rather pretty.

"Meg, I always knew you would be coming back one day, that you just couldn't stay away from this wickedly charming stepcousin of mine." Stephanie tapped Jon lightly on the arm and smiled flirtingly at him.

He looked annoyed, but Stephanie rattled on. "Meg, what's this I hear about you running a junk shop? I can't believe it. You were always so—so timid. I can't imagine you out and dealing with the public."

"I've been on my own over a year now since my aunt died," said Meghan with as much dignity as she could muster.

"Sorry about your aunt. I meant to get in touch, but it was about the time Daddy..." She went off into a lachrymose tangent then about her father. As her tears flowed, she leaned over to cry on Jon's shoulder.

"There now," he said, giving Stephanie a pat on the head and setting her away from him.

She loudly sniffed back her tears and tried to smile at Meghan. "I'm sorry. It's just that I miss Daddy so."

"I understand," said Meghan, feeling sorry for her.

Roland Deverell had been a sweet man and no doubt a good father to Stephanie and now all the poor girl had left was that mother of hers—Zena.

"Sorry to rush off, but I really have to be getting along now—have a bit of a drive ahead of me," Meghan said.

"Oh, you're not staying?" Stephanie looked round-eyed with surprise.

"No, I'm afraid I have to get back to ye old shop," said Meghan. She supposed later on she and Jon would tell the family about their on-again engagement. Right now she could hardly believe it herself.

In the kitchen Zena and Terrence were nowhere to be seen and Flory was putting the finishing touches to lunch. She looked disappointed on hearing Meghan was not staying.

"Everything smells so good, I wish I were. But I really have to be getting back."

Jon helped her into her coat, his hands lingeringly lifting her hair from the collar.

But Stephanie was eager to have Meghan go and waved her fingers at her. "Ta-ta, come back to see us."

Meghan smiled to herself at the insincere invitation. If all went well, she would in a few months be coming back to stay.

Outside, it was still gray and drizzly, but because Jon's arm was around her, it could have been a sunny spring day.

However, Meghan could not resist turning a questioning, half-teasing look at him. "Zena said Stephanie has been a great help to you."

"Stephanie's a big nuisance," he said.

Meghan was satisfied. How could she have been even a little jealous when with every step over the sodden backyard his lustrous eyes told her he loved her?

"When can I see you again?" Jon asked as they passed under the dripping, dangling willow. "What about tonight?"

"Oh, Jon, I don't think so. I'll be seeing Harley this afternoon. And then, with all this driving back and forth, I'll be worn out." She felt a little drained even now.

"Then tomorrow night," he said eagerly. "And I'll come bringing roses in one hand and chocolates in the other."

"And I'll make dinner for you," she promised.

"You mean you've learned to cook?" he asked incredulously.

"Aunt Duffy taught me," Meghan said proudly. "What would you like?"

"You," he said softly.

"No, to eat."

"What's your specialty?"

"Pot roast."

"Then make it pot roast," he said.

At the station wagon, they turned to each other and were embracing in one sweeping motion.

"Meg, Meg, thank heaven you've come back."

"I've missed you so," she said huskily. How could she have lived the last two years without him? But then she hadn't really lived.

"If only we didn't have to wait," he said. "So much can happen in six months—in six minutes, for that matter."

She saw the shading of fear in his face and knew a kind of dread within herself. Why did they feel so uncertain and apprehensive? Because of what had happened before, of course.

To shake off the sense of foreboding, she said fiercely, "Nothing can separate us again."

"We'll make it work this time," Jon said, equally resolute. Then he added with an anticipatory smile, "And what nice work it will be. Now what time tomorrow?"

"I close shop at five-thirty. Let's say six-thirty," she said. That would give her an hour to dress. She could put the roast and vegetables in the crock pot earlier.

"Don't go to a lot of trouble with dinner. You'll be the real feast for me," he said, pressing his lips to hers.

They tried to make it a kiss to last until they saw each other again, and her head was reeling when she finally slid behind the wheel of the station wagon. She wondered about driving while intoxicated with love.

He must have been concerned about that, too, for he cautioned her to drive carefully.

"We can't have anything happening now," Jon said, giving her a loving, desperate look.

And that was the look she took with her as she eased the station wagon down the drive. It troubled her that things had to be this way between them, that they were so afraid of something happening and being torn apart again. They were so overjoyed at planning a life together, but at the same time their happiness seemed such a fragile thing, a bubble ready to burst any moment.

"Please, God, don't let anything happen," she prayed. "I couldn't go through that torment again."

Back through the misting day Meghan drove, seeing little of the Tennessee countryside that was obscured by the drizzling rain as well as her tumultuous emotional state. How could she be so happily in love and yet so untrusting of the future?

Meghan arrived in Memphis at one and had a sandwich and glass of milk in the cafeteria of her favorite department store. She was too excited to eat all of the sandwich but drank the milk to have something to sustain her. She would need all the steadying strength she could muster when she told Harley.

But on leaving the cafeteria, she found she still had over an hour before she was to meet him and, as she wandered around the huge store, she could not resist doing a bit of shopping. She bought a flattering royal-blue dress to wear tomorrow night. And she also purchased a lot of frivolous stuff—perfume, fancy shoes, and costume jewelry to go with the new dress.

She got so carried away shopping, she lost track of time and was a little late getting to Ye Old Tea Shoppe where she was to meet Harley. It was a quiet, dark little place where they had often chatted away an hour or two and where he had proposed to her.

She felt guilty going in after buying so many items to make her alluring to Jon. She felt even more so on seeing Harley's worried face.

"I was afraid you weren't coming," he said, standing, a somewhat stocky figure at the tiny table. "I thought you may have just decided to stay at Blackthorn."

"Oh, Harley, you know I wouldn't do that without telling you," she said, sinking into the chair he held out for her.

Breathless after her shopping spree, Meghan faced him across the tiny table. Far too often she had looked at Harley without really seeing him, but now she was compelled to face him directly.

He had always been around and she was so used to him, she hadn't given him the proper attention at all. She hadn't noticed before how vulnerable his face could be. She hadn't noticed how nervous he could sometimes get. Harley was certainly tense right now.

She had come close to agreeing to marry this sweet, quiet, terribly serious man and yet she hardly knew him. How could she have done that? She had been driven by loneliness, she supposed, but how cruel of her not to think of him, his feelings.

Watching her with unwavering slate-gray eyes, he said slowly, "You don't have to tell me, Meghan. You've decided to go back to him, haven't you? I can see it in your face."

"I'm sorry, Harley," she said, feeling terrible, a beast, a very selfish young woman. She had gone out with him, leaned on him, and almost agreed to marry him, while all the while secretly loving someone else.

She was thankful the waitress appeared and Harley took his accusing, lifeless eyes off her. They ordered their usual—tea and scones.

As the waitress backed off, he turned again to Meghan, fixing that wounded look on her once more, and she could not help squirming, wishing she could run and hide somewhere.

"Well, Meghan?" he said, waiting with that awful patience of his.

She drew in her breath and came out with

it. "Well, we talked—Jon and I—and we decided to...to try again."

"I was afraid of that," he said bleakly. "I thought if you saw him again, he would persuade you to go back to him."

"I make up my own mind these days, Harley," she said gently but firmly.

"Do you—do you really?" He did not believe her. He thought she was still a puppet on a string, worked this way and that by Jon.

"Yes, I do," Meghan insisted. "But it's not completely settled yet. We want to wait six months before getting married. That way we'll give ourselves plenty of time to be sure. Oh, Harley, why didn't you tell me Jon had stopped drinking?"

"For two perfectly obvious reasons," he said. "One, I was afraid you would go rushing back to him. And, two, I didn't think he would stay on the wagon. I still have my doubts about that. He's sworn off before, you know."

"But he never lasted this long before," she said.

"You can't tell about alcoholics," Harley said with no malice in his voice. "I've heard about cases where they have abstained for twenty years, then—"

"Yes, yes, that's true," she said impatiently, not wanting to hear about those cases. "I know there's that chance, and that's why we're giving ourselves more time. But, Harley, there's also the chance Jon may never take another drink. He seems so much stronger, so much more mature now."

"The plain truth is, you still love him," Harley stated flatly. At the same time, there was an appeal in his look—he wanted her to deny it.

No need keeping him dangling.

"Yes, Harley, I suppose that is the plain truth."

He said nothing and there was desolation in his silence. His face was furrowed, his eyes like wet rock.

The waitress brought their tea and scones, but neither of them ate or drank for a long while. No light shone in the gloomy little corner of theirs. She should never, never have gone this far with him.

"You're not forgetting what Jon put you through before," Harley reminded her.

"No, I'm not forgetting. But, Harley, the only trouble we had was his drinking. We were happy when he wasn't drinking."

"And when was that?" he asked with irony.

"Well, before his parents died, of course. And even after that, he was sober most of the time. It was just that he could start to drink at any moment—and when he began, he didn't know how to stop. But that really didn't happen too often. And, anyway, he hasn't touched a drop in two years."

Harley drank a little tea and did not say anything for a moment. Then, with an air of finality, he remarked, "Of course, I'm through at Blackthorn. This washes me up good with the Deverells. Heaven knows I should have left long ago. Well, I was planning to leave, anyway. But now it would be impossible for me to stay. I'll leave as soon as I can pack and settle up."

"Harley, I hate to see you go. You've been there so long and everyone will miss you. And you really don't have to leave at all."

He lifted his bulky shoulders and let them fall. "Oh, it's time I struck out on my own. I'll find a small place for myself somewhere and, as soon as I'm settled, I'll let you know where. So if you ever need me, you'll know where to find me. You can always count on me, Meghan, you know that."

"I know," she said with a silent sob in her throat. Harley was playing Mr. Nice Guy right down to the finish. "You're a dear, Harley, the best friend I'll ever have."

"That's not exactly what I had in mind," he said, his eyes meeting hers, telling her how much he loved her.

"I'm sorry," she said.

He wanted no sympathy and said brusquely, "Let's get out of here."

As they were leaving the tearoom, Meghan glanced around, knowing she would not be coming back to it. She would miss the talks she'd had with Harley here, the companionship. Not only had he often advised and soothed her, but he had been a good listener as well. A friendly, reliable person—Harley. He'd never let her down.

Outside, he silently saw her to the station wagon. The drizzling rain of the morning had

finally stopped, but the day remained over-
cast, dreary. On the sunless sidewalk, they
said goodbye.

"For your sake, Meghan, I hope you'll be
happy with him." He clasped her hand in his
large, farm-roughened one. "Don't hesitate to
call on me if you should ever need me for anything."

He seemed to have strong misgivings about
her future with Jon.

"Oh, Harley," she said, close to tears.

"Goodbye, Meghan." He turned and hurried
down the dismal street, not looking back, his
trench coat flapping in the damp wind.

Deeply sorry for him, Meghan got into the
station wagon and headed for home. Because
she lived on the outskirts of town, and because
of the infernal rush-hour traffic, she was an
hour getting there.

The day had been such a mixture of highs
and lows, Meghan felt as if she had been on
a roller coaster and wanted only to get inside
Aunt Duffy's little house and collect herself.

Leaving the station wagon in the drive, she
hurried through the twilight to the cottage
standing shadowy and unlit in the juniper
bushes. As she started up the steps, loaded
with her packages, she heard the phone ringing inside.

CHAPTER SEVEN

Topped off with the threatening phone call, it had indeed been something of a day. Nevertheless, tired and upset as she was, Meghan reviewed it all. Everything she had done, said, everyone she had seen and talked to—all of it was gone over, sorted through. Somewhere in that day was the answer, she felt sure of it. Today she had touched a raw nerve in someone.

From habit she thought of calling Harley, but she quickly decided against it. She wouldn't bother him, not anymore. And there was the possibility, though distinctly remote, that Harley had made the call. But that would have been so very much out of keeping with his character.

He had ample reason to be angry with her, though. After dating him all these months and almost agreeing to marry him, she had told him she was going back to Jon.

But she could not by any stretch of the imagination see Harley making that garbled, menacing call, not good old, solid Harley. Best to leave him out of this, let him fade away in peace.

She would not call Jon either, for he would insist on coming into town and taking her back to Blackthorn. And it must not be settled that way. She would not go back to him in fear, in wild panic. When she and Jon got married, they would do it calmly. They had to start off right—make it work this time.

Again she considered notifying the police. Only recently she had read there were new methods for tracing anonymous callers. But she would have to tell them the whole story and they would tear the Deverell family apart, the family she was part of, the family that had done so much for her. And Jon could be a prime suspect because of his drinking past—and because she had been seeing another man.

Finishing the tea that had grown cold, Meghan scrambled a couple of eggs and made some raisin-bread toast. With a little food inside her, she might feel better, more able to deal with this. She needed to get the incident in the proper perspective. It could be she was giving too much importance to it. The caller might have merely wanted to frighten her, and that could be all there was to it. It could have been some prankster who'd randomly picked her name from the phone book. He or she had achieved his/her purpose, all right.

Her shoulders were still jerking convulsively.

When she had eaten the eggs and toast, she felt better, less hollow, not so jittery. Putting away her purchases, she curled up in Aunt Duffy's old bedroom, which she had turned into a den, and tried to concentrate on the ten-o'clock news on television.

Dido wound up in Meghan's lap and purred contentedly as her soft, creamy fur was stroked. What unworried, uncomplicated lives cats had, thought Meghan. They were not scared out of their wits by—

With the ringing of the phone, she jumped violently, startling Dido, who streaked off to a far corner of the room. Apparently Dido had had enough of Meghan. But whoever was on the phone hadn't.

On the fourth ring she went to answer. She could not stand it any longer. Maybe she could find out something. Shakily she picked up the receiver.

"Meg?" It was Jon's deep, caressing voice. Thank heaven.

In vast relief, she said, "Yes, Jon, I—I'm so glad you called."

He was silent half a second. "Meg, are you all right?"

"Of course. Why do you ask?"

"I don't know, but you sound nervous, not like yourself." He sounded puzzled, faintly anxious.

"Oh, it's been a very hectic day," she said, trying to sound casual.

"Was Harley difficult? You did tell him, didn't you?"

"Yes, I told him." She sighed wearily, thinking about her talk with poor, loyal Harley. She hadn't wanted to think about him again tonight.

"How did he take it?"

"Not well, but you know Harley. He didn't carry on or make a scene or anything like that. He was quite decent about it."

"You can trust old Harley to be that. But why doesn't he go find a new girl of his own?"

"Maybe he will now," said Meghan hopefully. "He must realize now I can never care about him, that way."

"The way you care about me?"

"The way I care about you," she said. "But, Jon, Harley says he'll be leaving the plantation very soon now."

"Good thing he's leaving the plantation," said Jon with unaccustomed vehemence. "I won't want him hanging around you. The sooner he goes, the better. I'm perfectly capable of running the place myself now."

"Of course, you are," she agreed.

"You're not just humoring me, are you?" Jon asked.

"No, of course not. I always knew you could—"

"Not then, Meg. I had to go all the way down before I could be trusted."

"Jon, you don't know how proud I am of you, the way you've pulled yourself up. I know it wasn't easy."

"You can say that again," he said with an uneven laugh and a sigh. "Oh, if you only knew! But we can take it from here, can't we, Meg?"

"Oh, yes, darling, I know we can."

"We'll talk about it tomorrow at dinner," he said. "I know you've had a tiring day. But I just thought I would call and wish you good night. And, Meg..."

Only he could make her shiver by saying her name. "Yes?" she said.

"I've been thinking about you all day. Like crazy. I'm like a kid again, waiting for Christmas, thinking tomorrow will never come."

"But it will—it will," she said. And everything would be all right.

"Sweet dreams, my darling." His voice was like a long, slow kiss.

"Good night, Jon." Meghan eased down the receiver and, hugging herself, waltzed around the room. Merely hearing him could spin her around with joy. And he wasn't drinking. He could not have made that awful call. How could she have thought for one minute that he could have!

Humming, determined to forget the anonymous call, she went into the bath to shampoo and roll her hair. She might not have time tomorrow.

When Meghan saw her stark white face in the mirror over the basin, she was shocked. She was so deathly pale. There was no denying the ugly incident had upset her and was still with her. Like some evil, persistent insect, the whispering, threatening voice circled around in her head. Her eyes, wide and shadowy with fear, were not really deceived—the phone call wasn't to be dismissed lightly. She knew those eyes in the mirror were staring at a victim, and her knees started shaking again.

But she mustn't let some goon do this to her. She and Jon were on the edge of happiness at last and some stupid phone call wasn't going to ruin it all. They would be married after a lot of heartache, and nothing must darken their hopes, their moment of triumph. Her mood should be one of gladness. Like a child waiting for Christmas, Jon had said. That was how he felt. She should feel like that, too.

When Meghan finally fell into bed, she was too exhausted, too tense, to sleep. Troubled, uneasy, she squirmed this way and that, unable to arrange herself comfortably. Her arms seemed to get in the way. And her head felt like a cabbage being shredded into fragments of fear and suspicion. All because she had gone back today to Blackthorn.

Someone out there hated her, hated her enough to snarl into the phone, "I'm going to kill you, Meg Latimer."

She shook her head on the pillow, hoping to drive out the echoing words. She would not think about it anymore tonight. She had to get to sleep.

Oh, dear, Mrs. Macklin's dog was beginning to bark. Was someone out there . . . after her? Well, maybe that ferocious animal would frighten off any prowlers or would-be burglars. If not, then perhaps it was her time to die. So be it.

Shifting it all over to Fate, she floated off to sleep. Afterward she wished she hadn't, for even in her dream she was stalked by her enemy. She was more vulnerable than ever in her light, restless sleep. It was strange, really weird. Dreaming, she knew who that enemy was, knew the person well, and the recognition jolted her awake.

Then she was unable to recall the face she had seen. The rest of the dream she recalled vividly. She was strolling down by the lake at Blackthorn when she became aware of footsteps stealthily trailing her.

Glancing over her shoulder, she saw a familiar figure, a known face among the beeches. She wasn't greatly alarmed until she felt the searing malignance of the eyes glaring at her through the gray, skeletal branches.

Twisting away violently, Meghan woke up, hearing herself sobbing, "No, no, not you, not you!"

Not who? Desperately she tried to recall the one she had seen in her dream, the one she knew so well. But whoever it was had fled, diving to the bottom of her subconscious, and lay buried now. Incomprehensible, she thought, the tears spilling down her face, the ache lingering in her throat.

Her surroundings started shaping up around her. In a dull sort of way, Meghan noticed thin shafts of morning streaking across her small room. Thank heaven the night was over. But she lolled on in bed, Dido warming her feet. Because she felt some measure of safety there, Meghan stayed put and mulled over the whole business. Here she was—knowing, yet not knowing. Asleep, she had seen the person with the hostility. Awake, she could not identify him—or her.

Although Meghan had misplaced the identity of the anonymous caller, she had not misplaced the caller. That person was still around, lying in wait. She felt sure of it with every bit of intuition she possessed. If only that intuition would pin a name on the scoundrel. How vexing—when in her dream she had known the individual almost as well as herself.

Unable to figure it out, she turned over, determined to snatch another forty winks. But Meghan was thwarted by the shrill ringing of the phone.

Sitting up in bed, she stared at the ugly black instrument. It was close, at her elbow. All she had to do was reach out, lift the receiver. But somehow she could not do it. She had the crazy notion she would be struck dead if she were to do so. That loathsome, venomous voice would do it. And it wasn't likely to be someone else. No one ever called her before seven in the morning.

Meanwhile, the phone went on ringing, shattering the peace and quiet of the small house, as it had done last night.

Finally, the piercing insistence of it was too much for Meghan and she picked it up on the seventh ring.

"Hello," she said in a thin, quavering voice.

"Miss Latimer?"

That didn't sound like that other person. All the same, she answered cautiously, "Yes, this is she."

"Hope I didn't get you up," Mrs. Macklin shouted, her voice passing straight through Meghan's head.

Suddenly Meghan loved her. She was a good old soul. Funny, thought Meghan, how she hadn't appreciated her neighbor before.

"No, Mrs. Macklin, you didn't wake me," she said, winking at Dido, that other sluggard. She wanted to laugh and cry with relief. Happiness was a loud old woman. May the world never be without next-door neighbors!

"Just thought I would call and see if you're all right," Mrs. Macklin yelled.

A chill swept around Meghan's shoulders and she paused in the act of reaching for Dido, who was climbing up her knees. Why shouldn't Mrs. Macklin think her all right?

"Why, yes, Mrs. Macklin, I'm fine." She scooped up the cat, holding her to her pounding heart. "Why?"

"Well, last night—actually, it was early this morning before daylight—Lorenzo started barking. I got up to see, and he was straining against the fence, looking in your direction. I thought about calling you but didn't like to, in case you were asleep and it was nothing, after all. As for calling the police, they don't pay any attention to me anymore when I call them. Or so it seems. But I thought I'd better call you first thing this morning and find out if there really was someone prowling around over there."

"If there was someone, I don't know anything about it," said Meghan, keeping her voice as steady as she could.

No need alarming the old woman by telling her about the anonymous caller. Mrs. Macklin was jumpy enough as it was.

"We women living alone can't be too careful. I still think you should get a dog, Miss Latimer."

"I may do that—if I stay here."

Mrs. Macklin caught her breath. "You're not thinking about moving, are you?"

"I'm considering getting married and going back to Blackthorn," said Meghan, the words sending joy rushing through her. "But if I do, I plan to rent out this house—so you'll have a close neighbor."

"Whoever they are, they won't be like you and Miss Duffy," said Mrs. Macklin stoutly.

Mrs. Macklin and Aunt Duffy had been great friends.

"And I'll never find another neighbor as good as you," said Meghan warmly.

"I'll miss you, but I'm glad you're going back to Mr. Deverell. I never thought he was as bad as everyone said he was. And it's a lonely old world living by yourself. Mr. Macklin was shiftless and no count, but never a day goes by I don't miss him. So you go ahead and try to work it out with your young man, Miss Latimer."

"I intend to," said Meghan.

"You do that, and good luck to you." She banged down the receiver.

With her ear resounding, Meghan did the same and went on sitting there, rubbing her chin across the top of Dido's purring head. She thought about Mrs. Macklin, but, no, it could not possibly be. Not Mrs. Macklin. She hadn't the motive, but she needn't have one if she were becoming deranged. She need only imagine Meghan had wronged her in some way. Perhaps stolen Aunt Duffy away from her. Mrs. Macklin might have even hoped Aunt Duffy would leave everything to her. Oh, that was ridiculous, paranoid. She mustn't start suspecting everyone.

Getting up, Meghan let the cat out and was amused seeing Dido prance along the fence, taunting Lorenzo, who strained against the wire, gnashing his teeth as he might have done last night. Someone might have been hanging around.

With a shiver, Meghan closed the back door. Then, passing through the house and shop, she stepped onto the front porch to get the paper. No footprints on the steps, no cigarette butts or evidence of a prowler.

As she turned to go back into the house, she

stepped back in dismay. "Oh, no!"

Thumbtacked on her door was a crude drawing of a skull and crossbones.

CHAPTER EIGHT

Angrily Meghan jerked the drawing from the door and stormed back into the house, her robe flapping around her bare ankles.

She would call the police now—she'd had enough. She did not care if it were someone "near and dear" who was up to these stunts. It was a matter for the authorities. She could not handle it alone. It was too much, too serious to take chances with, and in her hands she had proof she was being harassed.

Back in her tumbled bedroom, Meghan tossed the drawing on the bed and went for the phone, not stopping. This time she would do it, she told herself. But as her trembling hand reached out, she heard a knock on the door, the door she had taken the skull-and-crossbones drawing from only seconds before.

Standing very still, she gazed down at the face of the clock. Eight o'clock. Too early for

71

customers, too early for visitors, but not too early for a murderer.

Whoever it was seemed bent on tearing down the door. Squaring her shoulders, Meghan marched back through her small, shadowy house. She could have been a soldier, scared but going forth to meet the enemy. Her heart was racing so fast, the beats were tripping over each other.

Before opening the door, she stopped at the wide display window. From there Meghan had a good view of the front porch and, peeking through the old blue bottles, she saw what appeared to be a roly-poly bear puffing on a cigarette. Zena, all bundled up in her fur coat, was pounding on the door.

Meghan suspected at once that Zena had made the call last night, Zena had left the drawing, and Zena was now back to get her. It was not at all inconceivable.

Filled with qualms, Meghan opened the door. Zena was Jon's stepaunt. Meghan could not refuse to let her in. She could not sic the police on her either, not without a lot more proof than she had. She really had no evidence against Zena, only the knowledge that the woman hated her.

Drying her clammy hands on her hips, Meghan managed a weak smile. "Zena, hi. I'm glad to see you, but what on earth are you doing out so early? Nothing wrong at Black-thorn, I hope."

"No, I have an appointment with the hairdresser here in town at ten-thirty," she said, grinding out her cigarette with her high heel. "But I want to talk to you first."

And she charged in, scarcely waiting for Meghan to get out of the way. The exotic perfume she wore was too heavy, too powerful for so early in the day. So was she.

Forcing herself, Meghan invited her in. "Come on back to the kitchen, Zena, and we'll have a cup of coffee."

As they passed through the shop, Zena smiled condescendingly. "People will collect anything, won't they? Frankly, Meghan, I never thought you would get into anything like this."

"I don't understand it myself," Meghan admitted. "I suppose I more or less stumbled into it. But it's interesting. And people who buy this sort of thing are interesting, too. One will want a certain type of glass, another china, still another brass, and I have one customer who buys all the old tin she can lay her hands on. She paints on it."

My, she was chatty—nervous was the word.

Zena shrugged, not really interested. She had more important concerns than Meghan and her junk store. The kitchen was a bit crowded, but Zena sat down on one of the squeaky cane-bottom chairs. Slipping out of her fur coat, she glanced around.

"So this is where your Aunt Duffy lived. I never met her. I understand she didn't think much of the Deverell family." Zena, who had been a Grosbeck before her marriage, never considered herself anything but a Deverell.

"Aunt Duffy had her likes and dislikes. She was quite old, almost ninety when she died." Meghan doubted that Aunt Duffy would have liked Zena.

"And you've been living here alone since then? Don't you feel nervous staying by yourself?"

Turning the flame on under the coffeepot, her back to Zena, Meghan pondered the question. Zena could be feeling her out, finding out what the threatening call and skull-and-crossbones drawing had done to her. Meghan decided not to mention the incidents. If Zena were behind the pranks, she would probably give herself away sooner or later.

"Oh, I suppose I do get nervous at times," Meghan admitted. "And if I were planning to stay here, I would get a watchdog."

"Noticed your neighbor has a mean one," said Zena.

Meghan wondered if she had noticed that last night while pinning the drawing to the door. Zena was just mean enough to do those things.

Warily Meghan watched her take out her jeweled cigarette case, light another cigarette, and inhale deeply.

"So you're not planning to stay here?" Zena asked, her eyes narrowed on Meghan. "Going back to Jon?"

"Yes, but we're not rushing into marriage.

We want to give ourselves plenty of time."

"Good idea," Zena said. "You know, you two may not really be suited."

"Oh, but we are," said Meghan.

And while waiting for the coffee to boil, she sat down and faced the woman. Heavy makeup did not hide the hard lines in her face, and it was time she went to the beauty shop. Meghan could see the white roots in her red hair. Zena really would not have been a bad-looking woman if her expression were softer and she wouldn't make herself up like that.

But getting back to the subject at hand, Meghan said, "Really, Zena, why shouldn't Jon and I get back together now that he's stopped drinking?"

"That's the very reason why you shouldn't." Zena was studying her fingernails, as if debating whether or not to have a manicure while her hair was being done. "Jon has quit drinking, but if you two get back together, he might start again."

Meghan laughed, but there was no fun in it. "Are you implying, Zena, that he drank because of me, that I drove him to it?"

Zena looked up from her red-tipped hands and into Meghan's eyes. "All I know is, he didn't stop until you left."

The unfairness of the woman's reasoning cut Meghan deeply. Zena had always known how to deliver a mean blow.

"Zena, you know there were factors in Jon's background that might have influenced him to start drinking. His mother and father dying so suddenly. That was a terrible blow to him. And no one really knows what causes alcoholism. But I think there was something in Jon himself that he had to work out, which he seems to have done. So I see no reason why we can't get back together, why we can't be happy. Anyway, it's something Jon and I will have to settle."

Zena said, "You think that I'm meddling, don't you? That I should butt out? All right, let me tell you this. It does concern me because it concerns my child."

"Terrence?" Her son would not be likely to inherit Blackthorn if Meghan and Jon married, had children.

"No, Stephanie," said Zena.

Meghan stared at her and waited for her to explain.

"As I said before, she and Jon have become very close while you've been away and I believe she helps him whereas you..." She let her words die off.

Meghan shook her head and clung to Jon's explanation—that Stephanie was often a nuisance. Besides, though they weren't related by blood, he thought of her in a cousinly way, nothing more.

Zena was simply trying to make a good match for her daughter. If Stephanie married Jon, she would have Blackthorn. Then Zena and Terrence could stay there indefinitely. Parasites all three.

"Zena, Jon just doesn't love Stephanie that way," Meghan said.

Zena shrugged. "All I know is that they've been drawn to each other and get along very well together."

Meghan shook her head again. "Even if I hadn't come back to him, I doubt Jon would ever have married Stephanie."

Zena dragged deeply on her cigarette, her face harder than ever. "You've got it all figured out, haven't you? You think you can walk out on him whenever you feel like it, then come waltzing back anytime you want and take up where you left off. Pretty sure of yourself, aren't you?"

"I know Jon loves me."

Zena sat there in the smoky pollution she had brought into the kitchen, her eyes nailed on Meghan. "I can't see it, why he would prefer you. You're not as pretty as my Stephanie to my way of thinking."

Before nine in the morning, and after a bad night, Meghan supposed she didn't look so ravishing, especially in her old robe, with her hair in rollers. It was a good time to discount physical beauty and she did so with a jutting chin.

"What do looks have to do with love, true love?" Meghan demanded.

Zena, hanging over the sides of the chair, was no beauty. Still, Meghan would have loved her—if she hadn't been so hateful. Meghan had always wanted to love Jon's aunt.

"Love," murmured Zena skeptically. "Was it love that prompted you to walk out on Jon when he needed you most?"

"Yes, Zena, it was. If I hadn't loved him so much, I would have stayed and watched him destroy himself." With that Meghan stood up to see about the coffee. It was boiling and she poured two cups and handed one to Zena.

Jon's aunt sipped thoughtfully. "Shouldn't that great love of yours now keep you away from him when he's doing so well on his own? Why can't you let well enough alone? You've got your little business here and seem to be doing well. Why come back and stir things up again?"

"I'm not aware I ever did stir things up," said Meghan coolly, evenly. "But, Zena, you may as well know that if Jon and I do decide to marry, we will."

"In spite of how much Jon and Stephanie mean to each other—all she's done for him?"

"I'm glad if she's helped him, but Jon and I love each other. We always have and always will," said Meghan. Nothing could change that.

Zena stood up and slipped into her fur coat. "I wish you would think over what I've said. You and Jon didn't work out before and I doubt you will this time."

Meghan saw her to the door. "Goodbye, Zena."

"Take care," Zena said over her shoulder and headed down the walk to the old model Cadillac parked at the curb.

Closing the door, Meghan remembered the hideous drawing but still did not call the police. Perhaps she had gained confidence through Zena. If she could deal with that she-bear, she could deal with anyone.

And she became very busy. Meghan had no time to bother with pranksters. Singing loudly, she showered, dressed, and opened the shop. People came in and she waited on them, selling a pair of brass andirons, an old, beat-up cookbook and two snuff boxes.

The morning flew by and she was glad. Only a few more hours until her date with Jon.

CHAPTER NINE

After lunch Meghan had another customer or two. Then the day clouded over, and about three it started to rain, hard. It was not the fine, misting rain of the day before but a flooding downpour, and business slacked off to nothing.

For a while Meghan occupied herself cleaning a brass bed. Strenuous work that, and she didn't want to wear herself out. She wanted to be fresh for tonight.

When it was almost four, she put the roast in the crock pot. Jon was never one for eating rare roast, and she wanted it well-done for him.

Since the rain was still streaming down, she locked up the shop, showered, and slipped into her new dress. She would be ready in case he came early.

As Meghan finished doing her hair, someone knocked on the shop door. Despite the rain, a pair of dealers were out beating the bushes, looking for a bargain. Something for nothing was more like it.

But there now, she told herself. You don't want to become cynical, as one can so easily become in this business.

Actually, she was glad to have the dealers around, even though they were a sinister-looking pair. Better them than no one. After the harassing incidents, she wasn't too keen on being alone, and the gloomy afternoon was sinking into even gloomier twilight.

The dealers haggled a bit but bought the brass bed, although she had only half cleaned it. They were loading it onto their truck and Meghan was ringing up the sale when Jon drove up. Glancing at the one clock that ran in the shop, she smiled. He was early—eager.

With a singing heart and light, quick step, she went to the door and flung it wide for him. Still smiling, she watched him cut through the rain, his long legs flying over the puddles in the walk. Meghan thought he made a fine, lithe figure—romantic and dashing. He had a hint of the gentleman about him, a courtly touch of the Old South.

Jon saw her standing there, waiting for him, and his teeth gleamed in his wet, dark-skinned face. Only as he came up the steps and she saw him closer was the scar visible, but it did not matter. He was truly elegantly handsome.

"Come on in before you drown," Meghan said, pulling him inside. She almost wanted to cry. She loved him so much and was so happy.

"No one on earth would bring me out in such weather but you," he said, and there was a luster in his eyes.

But his shadowy cheek merely grazed hers in greeting. He could not have embraced her, anyway, not with his full hands. He held his gifts out to her—rained-on autumn flowers and a box of chocolates.

"Jon, Jon," she exclaimed, plunging her face in the clean, pungent marigolds. They came from home—Blackthorn. Flowers often bloomed there until almost Christmas.

"I picked them myself," he said.

"And they're all the more beautiful for that." She kept her face buried in the bouquet, not wanting him to see the sentimental tears in her eyes.

"So this is what you do," Jon said.

She looked up then and furtively wiped her lashes. He was glancing around the shop, taking in the colored bottles in the window, the wicker settee, the bean pots and flatirons in a corner, the clocks, the china cabinet filled with glass and bric-a-brac, the baskets and shelves of books.

He rocked on his heels. "I must say, you have quite an array of this and that. And your business must be good for them to come out in this weather. I saw them hauling away the bed. Meghan, I'm proud of you. You know, I always thought you beautiful, but now I'm pleased to find you're such a capable person, too. It's almost too much all in that one-hundred-ten-pound frame. And that brings me to...that pretty dress you're wearing."

"Like it?" She spun around and modeled it for him.

"You're what makes it," he said admiringly.

"Thank you," she said and added rather shyly, "Let's close shop and go on in back."

"Let's."

She locked up, turned the OPEN sign to CLOSED and left on one small light. Then she led him back to the living quarters. In the small dining area, she arranged the marigolds on the table she had set earlier with Aunt Duffy's best china and silver.

"There now, the flowers add just the right touch, don't you think?" Meghan asked, turning to him.

"Meg, Meg." He pulled her to him, kissing her wildly, ardently.

Alone as they were and with the rain pounding down the cottage roof, it was a moment of high bliss. Never had the flame of their love burned brighter.

It was all she could do to draw back from him, not be carried away. "I—I'd better see about the roast."

In the kitchen, as she lifted the roast onto a platter and arranged the carrots and potatoes around it, she said whatever came into her still-dizzy head. "No doubt this kitchen seems small to you after the one at home. It did to me at first."

"I'm glad you still think of Blackthorn as home," Jon said, lounging in the doorway, watching as she puttered around the room, taking rolls from the oven and butter from the refrigerator. "But, you know, this isn't bad. It's snug and cozy for this rainy night. Say, anything I can do to help?"

"Yes, carry in the platter and I'll bring the rest."

Back in the living-dining room, they arranged the food on the table. And then, as Meghan was lighting the candles, the phone rang. Ominously, she thought, remembering with chilling vividness the horrible menacing voice. She froze and, above the flare of a candle, he saw her face whiten and her eyes widen and darken with fear.

"Meg! What is it?" he asked anxiously, reaching over to grasp her wrist.

She moistened her lips. "I had a threatening call last night."

"Let me answer it," he said grimly. "Where's the phone?"

"Bedroom," she said, pointing to the door.

He went in but, before he got to the phone, it stopped ringing. Meghan by then had composed herself a bit.

"Oh, it was just probably someone wanting a pewter mug or something," she said as lightly as she could.

But he was not fooled. "Now what about the threatening call? Is it the first you've had?"

She nodded. "Yes, and I shouldn't have got so upset by it. Let's not let it spoil our dinner."

He sat down at the candlelit table but no longer appeared in a romantic mood. He was tight-lipped and had concerned lines between his eyes.

"What exactly was said?" he wanted to know.

She shrugged. "Oh, a lot of garbled stuff."

"But you said it was threatening?" he reminded her.

"Yes, he did say he was going to k-kill me," she said, swallowing hard.

"You didn't recognize the voice?"

She shook her head. "I couldn't even tell if it was a man or woman. The voice was disguised, of course."

"Meg, I never liked the idea of your staying here by yourself. You read of so many things happening. Why don't you close up the house and store and come home with me? Your old room is waiting for you—and you'll be coming back in a few months, anyway. Think how great it will be—our being together like this every day."

"Jon, I'd love to, but—"

"But what, darling?"

"It's not easy just pulling up and—"

"Better that than staying here and living in fear—and worse," he said.

"I—I haven't told you everything," she said. "This morning there was a skull-and-crossbones drawing on my door."

"That settled it; you're coming home with me," he said firmly. "But first let's have this feast you've prepared. You know, since I quit drinking, I have a giant-sized appetite."

Then they both endeavored to make it the romantic dinner they had planned, but all the while Meghan was aware of a tension in the air. They were merely making conversation, going through the motions of eating while their thoughts were on the anonymous call and the drawing.

He mentioned seeing the cat on the bed when he went in to answer the phone and teased, "You weren't settling down to being a spinster lady, were you?"

"Dido was Aunt Duffy's," she said. "And I was considering—not seriously—marrying Harley."

"Ah, yes, Harley," he said with a grimace. "Say, you don't think it could have been good old Harley who called. I wouldn't blame him for feeling put out."

She shook her head. "It would have been so out of character."

As they were starting on the chocolate pudding, she said, "By the way, Zena dropped by this morning."

"Zena? What did she want?"

"She said she thought it would be a mistake for us to get back together."

"Did she say that?" He looked annoyed.

Meghan nodded. "I think she wants you for Stephanie."

"She must be a fool and blind as well not to see I'm crazy, head-over-heels in love with you," Jon said with a shine in his eyes reflecting his words. "Oh, and that reminds me—I've brought something that should end all speculation."

He took from his pocket the large diamond ring he had given her when they were engaged before.

"My engagement ring," she cried, as if it were a long-lost friend.

He leaned across the table and, steadying her trembling hand, placed it on her finger.

"There now, that makes it official—we're to be married, if I don't make a fool of myself. But the way I feel now with your radiant face before me, I don't see how anything from a bottle could make me fly any higher, be any happier."

Eating only half the pudding, he pushed back his chair and Meghan could see the impatience in his face.

"Now, get your things together. You're coming home," Jon said.

"You mean tonight?" she asked incredulously.

"Hell, you don't think I'd let you stay another night here alone? Come on, I'll help you pack."

She put what she could in a large suitcase. She would have to come back later for the rest of her things. As he fastened the suitcase for her and she gathered up Dido, she knew a wild kind of elation.

It was happening. She was going home! But at the same time in some corner of her head,

Meghan knew everything would not be just fine there. She could be flying not away from the storm but straight into the eye of the hurricane.

CHAPTER TEN

Before leaving, Meghan and Jon checked everything in the small house, making sure all windows were securely fastened, no heat left on, all lights out. They could come back later and clean out the refrigerator. She would have to decide what to keep and what to sell of the furnishings, china, and the like. There was so much to do in the closing up of a house.

As they passed through the shop, Meghan felt no deep regret at leaving it. She was proud of what she had done here all on her own. But she would find new work at Blackthorn, and her love was there.

Locking up, they darted through the dark, chilling rain. Because the cat hated rain, Meghan held her under her raincoat where she purred contentedly against her heart.

Jon flung the suitcase in the back seat, helped Meghan in, and ran around to his side.

He pulled away from the shadowy cottage and they were on their way.

Nothing much was said until they were on the wet highway.

Then Jon spoke. "Meg, I want you to tell me the truth now. Do you have any idea, any idea at all, who could have made that call and left the drawing?" His eyes were on the slippery highway before them, but she knew his thoughts were on something much more treacherous—someone who wanted her dead.

"Well, I thought today it might be Zena," she said.

"Did it sound like her?" Without drawing his attention away from his driving, he turned ever so slightly toward her. His profile was somber in the semidarkness of the car.

"Jon, it didn't sound like anyone I ever knew," she said with a shudder, forgetting the faint familiarity she had detected in the spacing of the words, the subtle nuances. "If it is someone I know, he or she certainly did a good job disguising his or her voice."

"You couldn't tell whether it was a man or a woman?"

"I honestly couldn't tell. Whoever it was spoke in a whispery, husky voice and said things women don't usually say. But, of course, it could've been a woman who wanted me to think it was a man." She thought, We're putting this in the past tense, but it isn't over yet.

"Darling, you're shivering," he said. "Let's

not think about it anymore tonight. It could be over and done with, anyway. Now that you're coming home, you probably won't be harassed anymore. Just rest your head on my shoulder and try to sleep."

It was the best place she knew to rest a tired, bewildered head, but she had no more than closed her eyes than Jon resumed the conversation, as if compelled, as if intrigued beyond himself. "One thing I can't understand, darling."

"What's that?"

"Why in the name of common sense didn't you call someone, like the police—or me?"

"I was hoping it wasn't really anything— some kid I wouldn't hear from again."

"And after the drawing?"

"I was scared then and I started to call the police, but Zena came. Then I got busy."

He was not satisfied. "Did you think it might be someone in the family, someone close to you? Were you thinking of us, Meg? Were you trying to protect us?"

"I was afraid there might be some sort of investigation, that the family could be questioned. I didn't want to put you through anything. All of us have been through enough already."

As soon as she said it, she wished she hadn't. After his father had accidentally shot himself, police had swarmed all over the place and reporters, too. She hated reminding him of that sad, bewildering time.

Glancing at Jon's shadowy, morose face, she suspected he had been cast back into the guilt and torment of those days. He wore his old moody look.

She pressed closer to him. "Darling, darling, all we have to do now is look to the future."

"Yes, it's going to be all right now," Jon said, kissing her lightly, quickly, on the forehead. "Now that we're back together."

By the time they reached the gates of Blackthorn, it was deep into the night. Her head, still half-sleeping on Jon's shoulder, scarcely took in the fact. Meghan seemed to have fallen back in time, to another year.

It had been storming then, too, and, as they approached, wind suddenly blew one of the iron gates to. She had screamed, but it was too late—the car would not stop. It went crashing through the wrought-iron bars. It had looked to be almost deliberate on Jon's part, as if he had wanted to get into an accident. But, fortunately, neither of them had been hurt. Not physically. Yet it had been a nightmare then, and it was a nightmare now.

"Wake up, sleepyhead, we're home," he said, not sounding at all like that old Jon. That drunken, death-wishing Jon did not exist now, or the weak, tormented Meghan. They were two different people with a new life to live. They had to give themselves another chance with no harking back, no recriminations.

Sitting up straight and brushing her hair back from her eyes, she looked through the wild black night for the house, not always a haven in distress but at least something solid and a shelter. But now she was unable to find it. It lay hidden in rain, wind, midnight darkness, and clumps of trees. Spacious though it was, it could conceal itself. For a moment, she thought it had faded into nothingness.

But, no, there it was—exploding into fragments. The lights of the car advancing up the drive played on a long, darkened window, a pink brick corner, a soaring chimney. Like bits of bursting flesh, the house showed through tree, vine, weather, and night. It existed. And she would be safe there. She had to believe that. Here was the residence of her bone, flesh, and spirit, the dwelling place of her heart.

"Oh, Jon," she cried, laughing through tears. "I'm so glad—so glad."

He placed his hand warmly over hers. "So am I, sweetheart, so am I."

He pulled up under one of the wizened oaks and they piled out into the pouring rain and lashing wind. If Meghan's head was still a bit clouded with sleep, it cleared up then. Hugging Dido to her, she made a run for the porch, which seemed to her as big and overwhelming as when she had arrived as a child. She must remember to hold on to her newfound confidence and maturity. It wasn't easy, considering the things that had been happening.

Jon dashed up to the porch and muttered as he groped for his key, "They could have left the porch light on."

But the key turned out to be unnecessary, for the door swung open.

"Oh, Mr. Jon," exclaimed an agitated Flory, at first not seeing Meghan in the dimness. Then, catching sight of her, she looked even more upset, her eyes turning inward on some new fright. "Miss Meghan, Miss Meghan, you shouldn't have come, you shouldn't have come!"

"What are you saying?" Jon demanded. "Of course, Meghan should have come."

Flory shook her head vigorously. "No, no, she shouldn't. I've had this most terrible phone call warning her not to come to Blackthorn."

"Oh, lord," groaned Jon. "But let's get in, and you can tell us about it."

They went into the huge central hall and followed Flory back to the kitchen. There Jon set down the suitcase and Meghan turned Dido loose to go exploring her new surroundings. Meghan wished she could find some measure of well-being in the old country kitchen, but she could not, not with horror following her even here.

"I was having a little warm milk to quiet my nerves—I'll warm some for you, too," said Flory, moving distractedly over to the stove.

Meghan doubted warm milk would help much. It would not comfort them in a situation as serious as this.

"Sit down, darling," said Jon, holding out a chair for her.

Meghan sank onto it gratefully. Yet her legs

were as wobbly as when she had received her phone call.

"Now, Flory, tell us about the call," he said as Flory filled two mugs for them.

"It wasn't long after you left, Mr. Jon, late this afternoon. Mrs. Deverell hadn't come in from town yet, and Mr. Terrence and Miss Stephanie had gone out. Well, I'd put on the leg o' lamb and was starting on the pies—"

"For heaven's sake, Flory, skip all that and tell us about the phone call," said Jon impatiently.

"Yes, the phone call," she said, reminding herself, and Meghan noticed that the knuckles of her hand holding her mug were white and gleaming. Flory was scared to the bone. "I couldn't understand whoever it was at first. He didn't make any sense at all, but then gradually I began to get the drift of what he was talking about. He said I was to tell Miss Meghan that she was not to come back to Blackthorn under any conditions, that she would be in danger if she did."

Slowly, fearfully, Meghan looked across the table and into Jon's eyes, seeing her own fear reflected in his dark gaze. Silence screamed in the tall old rooms around them, and it was so quiet in the kitchen she could hear Dido lapping up the milk Flory had given her.

But outside it was still raging, with rain pounding against the black windows and wind howling like someone in torment.

Finally, Jon took a sip of warm milk, made

a face, and said, "In the old days, I would have laced it with bourbon and it wouldn't have been half bad. It would have been all bad—for me, anyway."

Meghan suspected him of trying to ease the tension, divert them from Flory's anonymous call, but she would not be diverted.

"Could you tell who it was, Flory?"

She shook her frowzy head while there seemed to be a shading of doubt in her face. "No, I don't think so. The voice was muffled in some way—horrible. And, oh, the things he said!"

"You say 'he.' You think it was a man?" inquired Jon.

"Oh, surely, a woman wouldn't talk that way," said Flory, shocked at the thought. But, after thinking it over, she added, "Well, I suppose some low, common woman might."

"You noticed nothing familiar about the voice, nothing to give him away?" asked Jon.

Flory hesitated with some discomfiture. "Well, I..."

"Yes, Flory, what?" he persisted.

"I was just going to say at first I thought I knew him, but when I'd had time to think about it, I didn't see how I could. I mean, no one I know talks like that, says such things."

"But he didn't threaten you?"

She shook her head and took a quick, nervous swallow from her mug. "No, he just threatened Miss..." She looked at Meghan as if she had forgotten her name.

"From now on, Flory, I'll try to answer the phone," said Jon.

"I wish you would," said Flory. "I know people get these calls and don't think anything about it, but this one was threatening Miss Meghan's life."

"And it sounded as if he really meant it, too," said Meghan, remembering her own call.

"Did you get one, too?" asked Flory.

Meghan nodded rather sickly. The calls weren't being randomly made. Someone was singling her out.

"Miss Meghan, did you think at first that you knew him?"

"Vaguely," said Meghan.

"All right, both of you, out with it," said Jon. "Who did you think it was?"

"I couldn't tell," said Meghan. "But I thought I ought to know him—or her. There was something familiar in the voice, in the way the words were spaced. I don't know what it was, but it was one reason why I kept on listening. I hoped the creep might give himself or herself away."

"Was it that way with you, Flory?" asked Jon, giving her an intent look.

She averted her face, looking ill at ease. "Not exactly, Mr. Jon. I don't like saying it, but when he first started talking, I thought— well, that you may have started drinking again and was playing some kind of prank on me."

"Was I ever, I ask you, in the habit of playing such a prank on you?" he asked. "Even when

I was rip-roaring drunk?"

"No, but—" Flory spread out her hands helplessly. "But one never knew what you'd do when you were drinking, and when you were a boy, you certainly were full of mischief."

"I think this is much more than mischief," he said. "But, Flory, for you to think for one minute that I—"

"Oh, I knew after a minute or two that it couldn't be you, Mr. Jon. You would never say those things, drunk or sober."

"Thanks," he said with irony. Then, managing another swallow of milk, he pushed back his chair. "But we can't do anything about this tonight and we're all dead tired, so let's just go on up to bed."

Flory clearly wasn't finished with the subject and asked as they stood up, "Who on earth would do such a thing?"

"Someone very sick," said Meghan, putting an arm around her tense shoulders.

"Or someone who would have us think that," said Jon, checking the back door, making sure it was not only locked but bolted as well. Then he picked up Meghan's suitcase. "Now, let's go up to bed."

At the foot of the back stairs, Flory turned an apologetic face to him. "Mr. Jon, I'm sorry I—"

"Oh, forget it, Flory."

But she would not let it alone. "So foolish of me when you've been doing so fine."

"Good night, Flory," he said tiredly.

She started up the dim, narrow stairs, then paused and looked uncertainly in Meghan's direction. "I'm glad you're back, Miss Meghan. It just hasn't been the same around here since you left. I hope nothing's—"

"Nothing's going to happen to Meghan," Jon interrupted. "Now please go on to bed. I'll check the front door."

CHAPTER ELEVEN

As Flory skittered upstairs, Jon shook his head, then seemed to forget about her as he reached for Meghan's hand. They walked up the wide, drafty hall and he set down her suitcase at the foot of the stairs. "I'll make sure the door's locked."

Her hand resting on the square newel post, she watched lovingly as his tall, lithe figure walked unwaveringly toward the front entrance. She thought how strange it was that both she and Flory had thought, though fleetingly, that the caller might be Jon. How could she love him so much and have flashes of mistrust? Was it impossible then to have absolute trust in another person? Knowing human weakness, could one have perfect faith?

Meghan shook her head as if to clear it of the unanswerable questions and any faint, lingering suspicion. She smiled as Jon returned to her, and he smiled back, his teeth flashing.

"There now, we're all locked up and the bogeyman shut out for the night," he said reassuringly.

As he took up her suitcase and they started up the winding old stairway, she had to believe it—that she was actually moving back in. Incredible but true. Slowly they went up the highly polished steps, not saying anything, not touching, and yet very much together in their old closeness.

They reached the top of the stairs and the dimly lit passage stretched out eerily before them. Meghan did not remember it seeming eerie in the past. And how the old warped floorboards creaked beneath their feet. There were so many paneled doors.

She wondered if anyone listened behind them. Not that door, though, she thought as they passed the master bedroom. It had been unoccupied since the deaths of Jon's mother and father. She could imagine it draped in sheets, ghostly.

Dido, as if nervous at being in a strange house, caught up with them and, when Jon opened the door to Meghan's room, dashed in ahead of them.

Jon turned on the light and placed the suitcase at the foot of the bed. Meghan glanced round smiling. Nothing had changed. It had been kept in order for her. The dark walnut furniture was all in place. The creamy bedspread and curtains were the same. All it needed was her hairbrush and makeup on the dresser, her books and pictures scattered around.

"I always knew you would be coming back. I had to believe that," said Jon, standing close behind her, his arms slipping around her waist. He lowered his face through her hair and kissed the side of her neck, and a shiver of delight ran over her.

She turned in his arms and they held on to each other in fierce desperation, as if they were to be torn apart at any moment. But they allowed themselves only one good-night kiss because of where they were and because of the intensity of their feelings.

"I'll see you in the morning," he said. "And, Meg, try not to think about that ugly business. We'll get it all cleared up. Don't you worry. Then we can go ahead with our wedding plans."

"Oh, Jon, do you really think it will happen—that we'll marry?" she asked, searching his face and eyes for reassurance. To have him was all she had ever really wanted, have the real Jon Deverell standing before her, not the unreal, unpredictable stranger of his drinking days.

"You had better believe it," he said, giving her a gentle shake. "Now, good night, my sweet."

"'Night," she said. She would believe it—they would struggle through to their happy ending. Not that it would be perfect—but close.

When the door closed behind him, Meghan lost no time undressing and falling into bed. Sleep was what she needed. Sleep would help her fight her doubts and fears. She wanted to hold on to the courage Jon had given her.

"You had better believe it," he had said. She would believe.

Dido curled up at the foot of the bed and they both slept in total exhaustion, scarcely moving.

The next morning, Meghan was glad to see it had stopped raining. Even though it was gray and Novemberish outside her bedroom window, she felt rested and glad to be home.

Dido wanted out and Meghan pattered downstairs in her robe and slippers to let her out. Then she ran back up to shower and dress, putting on good country clothes—jeans and sweater. She smiled, knowing she had the figure for them, smiled because Jon was back in her life to admire and love her no matter what she wore.

As she stepped confidently out to the passageway, she met Stephanie coming out of her room across the hall.

"Hi," Meghan said.

"So you've come back," said Stephanie, not returning her smile, looking as if she had been crying. She was pink and puffy around the eyes.

She must have been more serious about Jon than Meghan had thought. She might have thought she was making progress with him, and now her plans were dashed. Meghan could not help feeling sorry for her. She knew how she would feel if she lost Jon to someone else.

But Stephanie was pretty—she would find someone else. Maybe she and Harley—Stephanie had once seemed interested in him. Although she didn't seem his type...

"Yes, I'm back," said Meghan, not knowing what else to say.

"And I suppose you and Jon will be trying it again—to get married?" Stephanie's round-cheeked face appeared skeptical.

"Yes, we're planning to be married in a few months," said Meghan as they moved along the creaking hall to the service stairs.

"I just hope Jon continues to do well. He hasn't had a drink since you've been away," said Stephanie.

How like her mother she was under all her girlish prettiness, thought Meghan. Oh, dear, it wasn't going to be easy dealing with both of them.

"I have faith that Jon will be the fine, strong person he was meant to be," said Meghan as they started down the stairwell. She walked carefully, since it was steep and poorly lit and had no handrail.

"I'm wondering if you're good for him," said Stephanie, following close behind her.

"Why do you say that?" asked Meghan.

"Some people just aren't suited for each other," said Stephanie.

Within the narrow walls of the stairwell,

Meghan was conscious of the girl's hostility and jealousy, and was relieved when they reached the bottom of the stairs.

"I'm sorry you feel the way you do, Stephanie," she said. "I was hoping you and your mother and I could all be friends, that you would give Jon and me your blessings."

"I'm afraid that's impossible. You see, Meg Latimer, you don't fit in here and you never have. You don't know how peaceful it was while you were gone. Everyone getting along, no rows between you and Jon."

Angrily Meghan turned to face her. "Stephanie, you know we quarreled only because of his drinking. I couldn't bear to see him destroying himself."

"You don't know how to handle him," said Stephanie smugly.

"And I don't intend handling him—Jon is perfectly capable of taking care of himself," said Meghan. "Now I'd better see about my cat before those hounds get to her."

Leaving Stephanie pouting there in the hall, she hurried to the back door. Looking out, she found Dido struggling not with the hounds but with something fastened about her neck.

"What on earth—?" Meghan knelt down to untangle the black gauzy material that was driving Dido into fits. When she finally got it off and examined it, she saw that it was a mourning veil.

As she stood staring at it, Terrence came whistling across the sodden grass, the hounds at his heels.

"What goes?" he asked, holding back the dogs.

"I found this tied around her neck," said Meghan, holding up the veil. "Do you know who it belongs to?"

He gave it a desultory glance and shrugged. "Looks like something Mother wore to Dad's funeral. But what was your cat doing with it?"

"More to the point, who tied it around her neck?" snapped Meghan, scooping up poor confused Dido and stalking back into the house with her.

CHAPTER TWELVE

Passing through the kitchen, Meghan stopped to ask Flory, "Do you know anything about this? See anyone with it? Or how it got around Dido's neck?"

Flory turned from the stove, and her pale, vague eyes widened and sharpened at the sight of the gossamer material Meghan held out for her to see.

"Around your cat's neck? But that's Mrs. Deverell's mourning veil."

"I know and some lunatic tied it around Dido's neck," fumed Meghan.

"Could've been somebody's idea of a joke," said Terrence, who had followed her in.

"A sick joke, if you ask me," said Meghan.

Leaving Dido in the kitchen and going on to the breakfast room, she found Zena pouring coffee and Stephanie already seated at the table.

"Why—why isn't that my veil?" asked Zena, surprise showing in her face.

Of course, she could have faked the surprise, thought Meghan. After all, the veil belonged to Zena.

"I believe it is yours—it was fastened around my cat's neck," said Meghan coolly.

"Your cat's neck?" asked Stephanie, trying not to smile.

"I don't think it's one bit funny," said Meghan.

Zena set the coffeepot down, snatched the veil, and brushed the cat fur off it. "If someone's playing jokes, I wish they would leave my things alone."

"And I wish they would leave my cat alone," said Meghan. "Dido could have been strangled by that thing."

"That thing happens to be the veil I wore to dear Roland's funeral," said Zena, holding it to her large bosom. "And this means someone has been in my room, rummaging around in my cedar chest. Terrence, you wouldn't—I mean, you're surely too old for such nonsense?"

"Yes, Mother, I'm too old for such nonsense," he said. "Anyway, I've been out walking the dogs."

Walking the dogs or not, he still could have done it, thought Meghan.

"Stephanie?" Zena turned a questioning look upon her daughter.

"No, Mother," said Stephanie, as if her patience was strained. "I didn't do it, and I don't see why there's all this fuss about it. It seems like a harmless little joke to me."

"What's a harmless little joke?" asked Jon, entering quietly.

Seeing him, Meghan almost forgot for a moment the veil incident. He was fresh from his shower, his dark hair curling on top of his handsome head, and he brought with him the spicy, manly scent of after-shave. Even in Levi's and a flannel shirt, he looked like a prince.

In her admiring, adoring silence, she left it up to Zena to explain.

"Oh, someone tied my mourning veil around Meghan's cat."

Jon was not amused. "All right, Stephanie and Terrence, which one of you idiots did it?"

"Jon, you know I wouldn't do a dumb thing like that," said Stephanie, looking wounded.

Jon glanced at Terrence, who raised his right hand and pleaded, "Not guilty."

He turned a silent, questioning look at Zena.

She drew herself up indignantly. "You surely can't think that I—and with the veil I wore to poor Roland's funeral?"

"I don't know what the devil to think," said Jon. "But I won't have Meghan or her cat harassed this way. I want that understood right now."

"Maybe Flory did it," said Stephanie.

Flory, bringing in a platter of bacon and scrambled eggs, overheard her and declared,

"No, I didn't! I love animals and wouldn't treat one that way for the world."

"I know you wouldn't," said Meghan.

But, as Flory slammed the platter on the table, Meghan wondered if she really knew Flory or anyone else in the room except, of course, Jon. She knew him well enough to know he wouldn't torment a cat that way.

"No one else has been in the house, so it must have been one of you," said Jon.

"Well, it wasn't me," said Flory, whisking back to the kitchen.

"What about old Harley?" grinned Terrence, only half serious. "He could be sore because Meghan dumped him."

"Harley would never do such a stupid thing," said Meghan.

"Anyway, he hasn't been in the house this morning," said Jon.

"He was yesterday afternoon, looking for you," said Stephanie. "He could have sneaked upstairs then and got the veil."

"Harley was looking for me?" asked Jon with a lift of one eyebrow.

Stephanie nodded. "I think he wanted to hand in his notice."

Flory, returning with hot biscuits, said, "And if you all think I put that thing on the cat, I'll hand in my notice, too."

"Flory, no one is saying you—" Jon began.

"She did," said Flory, pointing at Stephanie.

"I didn't really mean it," said Stephanie. "I was only joking, for heaven's sake."

"No more joking," said Jon. "And no more

harassing Meghan. Now let's have breakfast and we'll discuss this later."

Looking not quite mollified, Flory returned to the kitchen and Meghan began to go through the motions of eating.

"I'll say one thing," said Terrence, buttering a biscuit and smearing it with pear preserves, "You sure bring the excitement with you, Meg."

"Don't blame this on me," said Meghan. "The excitement, as you call it, was already here."

"Darling, try not to think about it now and eat your breakfast," said Jon gently.

And no one mentioned the incident until they had finished eating and were on their second cups of coffee.

Then Jon quietly turned to Zena. "I've been intending to ask you, Aunt Zena, if you've had any anonymous calls lately."

She stared at him and shook her head. "Why, no. Why?"

"Both Meghan and Flory have received threatening calls and I was wondering if you had."

"No, but then I don't answer the phone very often—Flory and Stephanie usually beat me to it."

"I had a crazy caller once," said Stephanie, shrugging. "It's nothing to get excited about."

"But these have been threatening calls," said Jon. "And there've been other incidents."

"You mean besides this incident with my veil?" asked Zena.

"Actually, there's been one incident besides

that one," said Jon and told her about the skull-and-crossbones drawing.

Zena listened intently, and Meghan could hear her breathing. When Jon finished, she leaned across the table and said softly, "I don't like saying anything. She has been with us so long. But Flory's been acting very peculiar lately."

"Flory has been weird ever since I can remember," said Stephanie.

"But she's been getting worse," said Zena. "Did you see how she slammed that platter on the table?"

"Well, I'd be angry, too, if someone had accused me of mistreating a cat," said Meghan.

"But there've been other things," said Zena. "She seems more absentminded and confused. And I've heard her in the kitchen talking to herself."

"Oh, Flory's always done that," said Meghan. "I remember when I was a child wishing I were old enough to talk to myself, too."

"Oh, well," said Zena, looking at Meghan as if she were an odd one also.

"Flory's a little befuddled at times, I know," said Jon. "But she's got a good heart in her— she would never play cruel tricks like these."

"She has never liked her," said Zena, flashing another look at Meghan.

"Her name is Meghan," said Jon. "And Flory has always been fond of Meghan."

"Not since she tattled on her and Edward," said Zena.

Jon frowned at the mention of his father.

"That was a long time ago, Aunt Zena," he said quietly.

"But Flory hasn't forgotten. I know she hasn't," said Zena, seeming anxious to pin the mischief on the cook.

That was understandable, thought Meghan. The Dido bit narrowed the suspects down to someone in the house, or at least someone on the plantation. In blaming Flory, Zena was trying to extricate herself and her darlings.

"But Flory got a threatening call herself," Meghan pointed out.

CHAPTER THIRTEEN

Before Meghan ran up for her coat, Jon advised her to bundle up good. "It's damp and cold out, and be sure to put on heavy shoes. The ground will be wet after all the rain."

In her room, pulling on knee-high boots, Meghan smiled to herself. He certainly was watching over her, and she loved it. After two years of being on her own, she needed a little tender loving care.

Draping a purple wool scarf around her head and buttoning up her coat, she hurried down to him. At the back door he was pulling a knit cap down over his ears. In that and a plaid mackinaw coat, Levi's, and Western boots, he looked outdoorsy and manly. A little like Paul Bunyan.

Outside it was, as Jon had said, cold and damp and sloshy underfoot. The sky was a dark gray bowl filled with nothing but ominous clouds. The trees were mostly bare and shivering. But Meghan felt invigorated at being out and drew a deep breath of the clean, sharp air.

As they cut across the backyard, she felt more than invigorated. She felt exhilarated at being back in the old familiar surroundings and being with him. This was where she belonged. She even delighted in seeing such everyday things as the pump house, the tractor shed, and the red, tin-roofed barn on the slope. But most of all, she delighted in having Jon at her side, his strong, exciting hand warming hers.

But her smile faded as they came in sight of the lake cottage with Harley's car parked in front of it. She wished they had gone another way. She did not want to chance running into Harley just now, not when she was so happy at being home. It would be like flaunting her new happiness before him.

"Let's go back through the orchard," she said.

"Too late," said Jon.

Harley was coming out of the cottage carrying a large box, evidently clearing out. He saw them and called to Jon, "I'd like to see you sometime today—when you're not busy."

"I'll be back in about an hour," said Jon. "We can settle up then."

Harley nodded, his square face solemn and unsmiling, and Meghan noticed he had a scratch on his chin, as if he had cut himself shaving. She felt achingly sorry for him—he looked so alone.

"Hi, Harley," she said awkwardly. If they could simply be friends—that was the way it was meant to be.

He nodded briefly and went on loading the box in the trunk of his car.

"Oh, Jon," Meghan whispered as they moved around the lake. "He didn't even speak to me. He blames me and I don't blame him. I shouldn't have encouraged him, led him to believe I might marry him. It was a mean, cruel thing to do. I didn't realize my true feelings, but I should have."

"And he should have known better," said Jon, not showing too much sympathy. "He should have known that sooner or later you and I would get back together. He saw us together, saw how it was with us, and shouldn't have tried to come between us."

"But he must have thought it was all over with us," she said.

"Did you think that?" he asked, turning a searching look on her.

"I knew—when I came back here on Monday—I could never love him or anyone else the way I love you," she said. "But I should have realized it all along."

"I'll be glad when he's gone," said Jon impatiently. "Even before I found out about him sneaking around and seeing you, I never liked him. And it wasn't only because Father was always praising him to the skies and wanting to know why I couldn't be more like good old Harley. No, there was something else about him I didn't like—I think it was because he was too damned perfect to be real."

He stopped at the reedy edge of the lake and looked out over the gray, wind-whipped water. "Remember what great times we used to have out there?"

"Oh, yes." She smiled, leaning closer to him as she recalled those times. Swimming, boating, fishing—there had always been something to do on the lake. Even on cold, dreary days like this, they'd had fun casting pebbles or merely watching the ducks.

"We're going to have all that again," Jon promised, his head pressed against hers as they gazed out over the choppy water. "And our children will have what we had."

Our children, Meghan thought ecstatically. How wonderful that sounded, how wonderful it would be—raising a family here at Blackthorn. It seemed almost too good to be true, but she mustn't doubt. Of course, it would happen. Their dream would come true. It wasn't asking too much. She and Jon would marry, have children, live out quiet, peaceful lives here.

They continued their walk but were only halfway around the lake when they felt the first cold drops of rain.

"Blast it," he said as they started back. "And I wanted to show you how we've cleared some of the bottoms and I wanted to take you through the woods. Remember those grapevines and how we used to swing out over the creek?"

"And how I fell in," she reminded him. She could laugh now, but it hadn't been so funny then.

She had been scared to death swinging on those vines, but because Jon had dared, she had dared. And when they had gone to the house and Jon's father had seen her wet and bruised, he had scolded Jon, although she had insisted it was her own doing. Mr. Deverell had always been a little hard on Jon, but then Jon had been a handful.

"You haven't forgotten our tree house?" he asked. "Do you know that part of it is still there?"

"We'll have an active little boy and girl who will build another," she said. "Oh, Jon, what a wonderful place this is to grow up in—and to grow old in."

"And to think I almost threw it all away," he said, shaking his head, as if not comprehending himself or the person he had been. "But come on and let's hurry and get inside before we drown."

It was raining harder, and they hurried toward the house. When they passed Harley's forlorn little cottage, she was relieved he was nowhere in sight. She wondered, though, if he were watching them from one of the windows, watching her and Jon tear through the rain, hand in hand, their faces gleaming, unable to conceal their joy at being together again. Like Jon, she would be glad when Harley was gone. It would hurt him too much to stay, and she didn't want to see him hurt any more than he already was.

Dashing on to the latticed-in back porch, they were a little surprised to see Terrence sitting on the toolbox there, watching the rain.

"You didn't have much of a walk, did you?" he said almost gloatingly. "But that's the way it is at Blackthorn, always raining. You'll just have to get used to it again, Meg."

"Oh, we had rain in Memphis," she said, taking off her scarf and shaking the drops out of it.

"Anyway, the sun will always be shining for Meg and me," said Jon. "No matter what the weather is."

Then he turned to Meghan. "Honey, as long as I'm already wet, I'll just run on down and get everything squared away with Harley. I should be back in time for lunch."

He kissed her rain-washed cheek and went back into the rain. She watched until he disappeared behind bushes and the liquid sheet of weather. He wanted to get it over with, the business with Harley. It was bound to be unpleasant.

Meghan had almost forgotten Terrence lounging there until he spoke. "Hard to believe old Harley will be leaving us—won't be the same around here without him. He's kind of a fixture, but I guess Jon wants to get his rival out of the way as quickly as possible."

"Harley's not a rival," said Meghan. "He and I were just good friends in Memphis, but deep down I've never really loved anyone but Jon."

"Yeah, you two always were like peaches and cream," Terrence said. "Hope it works out for you this time."

He sounded skeptical.

"It will," said Meghan and started to go in but turned to give him a curious glance. "Aren't you cold sitting out there?"

"Better here than in there," he said, jerking his head toward the door.

"Why? What's going on?"

"Big scene in the kitchen," he said.

"Oh, dear," she said and went in to see for herself.

Indeed the kitchen was in something of an uproar with poor confused Flory running around in circles saying distractedly, "I'll brew her a cup of tea. Tea always helps."

Meanwhile, Stephanie sobbed uncontrollably, and Zena puffed on a cigarette and said to her daughter, "No, you can't—"

"What is it? What's going on?" asked Meghan anxiously, swooping up Dido, who was looking dazed.

"Stephanie says she's leaving," said Zena, glaring at Meghan as if it were her fault.

"Leaving?" repeated Meghan, noting the suitcase at Stephanie's feet.

"She says she wants to go to Memphis and get a job," said Zena, smashing out her cigarette with a vengeance. "She says she can't bear to stay here—now."

"I'm sorry," said Meghan. "But if that's her decision—"

"You'd like to see her go, wouldn't you? You'd like to see us all go. Then you could have it all and Jon, too," said Zena.

"I only want us all to get along and try to be happy," said Meghan with a deep sigh. That seemed impossible at the moment.

"Here's a cup of tea, miss," said Flory.

Stephanie wiped her face and took the cup. Meghan had the impression she was enjoying the attention she was getting, the stir she was causing. Over the rim of her cup, she fixed red-lidded eyes on Meghan.

Then, between sips and sobs, she ranted, "When I became interested in Harley, you took him. Then when I—I fell in love with Jon, you took him t-too. I just don't have a chance here. So I'm leaving and, Mother, you can't stop me!"

"If you'll just wait a day or two, you may feel differently," said her mother.

Stephanie shook her head vigorously, splashing tea in her lap. "No, I know I'll feel the same. I'd be miserable here now."

"Then wait until I can go with you and help you find a place to stay," said Zena. "But I want to tell you, I'll be worried every minute about you staying in Memphis all by yourself."

"Nothing happened to me while I was there," Meghan pointed out. True, she'd had that dreadful phone call and the skull-and-crossbones scare, but she was convinced those things emanated from Blackthorn.

"Maybe nothing happened to you, but Stephanie's younger and—" Zena left off saying prettier. In her opinion, every man in Memphis would be after her daughter. "We need to think this over, Stephanie, and not rush into anything. If, in a week or so, you still want to go, I'll drive you in and help you get settled somewhere."

Meghan smiled to herself as she went upstairs to change out of her muddy boots. Zena would never leave her precious lamb alone in the big city. But why the delay? If they were leaving, she wished they would go. She supposed, though, Zena would have a lot of packing to do—and perhaps some unfinished business here.

CHAPTER FOURTEEN

Getting into dry shoes, Meghan made her bed and straightened her room. Then she paced about, feeling restless, trapped by the steady, unbroken rain streaming down the windows.

She wished Jon hadn't gone out in it. She felt uneasy about him and would be glad when he was through with his business with Harley. It would be difficult for both of them. Making a change was never easy. She could imagine how strained the meeting would be. But it shouldn't take long. Both of them would want to get it over with.

When an hour had passed and Jon hadn't returned, she began to feel more than a little anxious about him. It was reminiscent of times in the past when she had waited and waited and waited for him, only to have him come in hours later staggering drunk. Now why were her thoughts drawn that way?

As if to escape her misgivings, Meghan went

down to the kitchen but only brought her apprehension with her.

"I can't imagine what's taking Jon so long," she said, peering out the window, trying to see the cottage but seeing only rain and the dark outline of trees and shrubs.

"Oh, I guess it takes time to let someone go who's worked as long as Mr. Harley has," said Flory, stirring a pan of creamy sauce.

It seemed they would be having salmon croquettes, but Meghan wasn't the least bit interested in food at the moment.

Glancing nervously at the loud-ticking kitchen clock, she said, "It's been almost two hours, Flory. What can they have to discuss that long?"

"Now, don't fret yourself, Miss Meghan. He'll be back any minute," said Flory, but she sounded to Meghan as if she were merely mouthing words, as if her mind was on something else.

She had always been rather absentminded, out of it. The only thing Flory really seemed to be able to concentrate on was her cooking. Thank heaven she wasn't forgetful when it came to that.

Trying to settle down, Meghan flopped on one of the kitchen chairs, sighing heavily. "What a morning it's been—with that mourning veil business and Stephanie saying she was going to leave. Do you think she will— or do you think Zena will talk her out of it?"

"As they were leaving the kitchen, Miss

Stephanie was swearing she was staying only a day or two longer so's her mother could come with her and help her find a place."

"I wouldn't be surprised if Zena decided to stay with her in Memphis," said Meghan hopefully.

Flory turned a smiling impish face on her and whispered, "Wouldn't that be nice?"

Meghan laughed and the tension was broken somewhat but not altogether. And when Jon still hadn't returned a half hour later, Meghan was down to gnawing her knuckles.

"What could be keeping him?" she wailed.

"Maybe they got in a fight down there," said Terrence, who had ambled in and was waiting around for lunch.

"Mr. Jon was never one for fighting—even when he was drinking," said Flory, doing her best to keep the food warm.

"I hope all this excitement doesn't start him to drinking again," said Zena, who had evidently been listening from the doorway.

"Jon is stronger than that now," said Meghan.

Zena shrugged, looking not so sure. "Let's hope so. Oh, Flory, I think I'll just fix a little tray and take it up to Stephanie. Poor child has a headache and doesn't feel much like coming down."

Meghan noticed that she prepared quite a large tray for someone not feeling well. But then perhaps she planned to eat with her daughter.

"I think I'll just go ahead and have one of those croquettes myself," said Terrence. "And a hunk of cornbread."

He ate the food there at the kitchen table, ate as if nothing was wrong, as if Jon hadn't been gone far too long.

Again Meghan glanced at the clock—almost two! She couldn't stand it any longer.

"I think I'll run down to the cottage and see what's keeping him," she said.

"You think that's smart?" asked Terrence, reaching for another croquette. "After all, you're the bone of contention. They might really tear into each other if you go down there."

"And it's still pouring rain," said Flory.

"I don't care. I have to find out what's happened to Jon," said Meghan over her shoulder as she left the kitchen.

She flew up the service stairs, two steps at a time, raced to her room, changed back into her muddy boots, and threw on her damp coat. All the while her head spun with one question: What could be keeping him? Jon said he would be back in time for lunch and it was way past that now. What could be keeping him down there?

It was true that in the past Jon hadn't always kept his promises, but he had been drinking then. He hadn't been drinking today, and he must know she would be worried with all the crazy things that had been happening. What could have detained him?

Losing no time, her coat flaring around her, Meghan rushed back downstairs, through the back porch, and plunged out into the harsh, nail-sharp rain. Oh, dear, she had forgotten her head scarf. Never mind, she had to get to Jon, see what was holding him up. She had the most horrible feeling something might have happened to him. Please, God, she prayed, not now when we're just getting back together.

She splashed across the backyard and struck out for the cottage. As she drew closer, she saw that Harley's car was still there. That meant he hadn't left yet, and he and Jon could be inside going over the necessary business of terminating Harley's employment. She had no idea what that involved and hoped there was no disagreement or misunderstanding.

Pounding up to the small porch, Meghan suddenly felt a little foolish, dashing out into the rain like this, looking for Jon as if he were an unreliable, runaway child. She was over-reacting, being unnecessarily concerned about him. In her agitated state and with her wet, straggling hair, she would surely appear hysterical, overwrought. She didn't care—she had to find out why Jon was taking so long, why he hadn't come back when he had said he would.

Even her knock sounded urgent, frantic, and she didn't blame Harley for looking surprised at the sight of her. But, oh, how solid and reliable he looked standing there in his conservative tweeds. She wanted to rush into his arms and lean her frightened, confused head on his broad shoulder. She resisted the impulse. No more of that. It wasn't fair to him. Anyway, she was here to see about Jon, that was first and foremost with her.

"Jon—he isn't here?" she asked breathlessly, hope fading fast in her.

"Why, no," said Harley, looking even more surprised. "He left here over an hour ago."

"An hour ago?" she repeated. What in the name of heaven was going on here? When she could speak, she asked, "Did he say where he was going?"

"Why, no, but I assumed he was going back to the main house. I really didn't pay much attention, though. I've been busy packing. Heaven, the things we accumulate."

She didn't want to hear about that and asked impatiently, "Where could he have gone in that rain?"

"Well, you know Jon. He has been known to wander before," said Harley with a trace of unexpected irony.

"But that was when he was drinking," she said, her voice going shrill. Why couldn't people understand Jon wasn't like that anymore?

He gave her a long, level look that said as plainly as any words: And he could be drinking now.

Aloud he merely said, "Old habits are hard to break sometimes."

Angered, she declared, "Jon's not going back to all that! There's got to be some explanation for this. He may even be back at the house now. Sorry to have bothered you."

"You never bother me, Meghan," Harley said softly, his gray eyes resting on her unwaveringly. "And don't forget. If you ever need me for anything, be sure to let me know. I'll send you my address and phone number as soon as I'm settled."

"I appreciate that, Harley, and everything you've done for me, but I think I'll be able to manage now," she said, wanting him to know she wouldn't be running to him with her problems, hanging onto him in helplessness and loneliness. She would not use him in that way anymore. It was all over with them.

Anyway, at the moment, all she had on her mind was Jon. Where could he have gone after leaving Harley?

Forgetting even to say goodbye to him, Meghan started back for the main house on the run. Scarcely aware of the cold rain pouring over her, she leaped at the possibility that Jon might have come in from the other direction and was at the very moment in the kitchen asking about her. He would be worried about her running around by herself after the threats she had received.

Panting, praying fervently he would be there, she ran in. But the minute she burst in and saw the questioning look on Flory's face, she knew he hadn't returned. Desolately she wondered again: Where was he?

CHAPTER FIFTEEN

Motionless, dripping rain on the kitchen floor, Meghan had to ask, although she already knew the answer, "You haven't seen Jon?"

Flory shook her head. "No, but, Miss Meghan, he could be anywhere on the place. He could've thought of something he had to see about. Mister Jon's very conscientious about what's to be done since he stopped drinking."

"Then he could have gone to the barn to see about the stock or something," said Meghan, snatching at anything, any thread of hope.

"I expect that's what's happened," said Flory soothingly. "Now why don't you get out of those wet clothes before you catch your death and come have a plate of lunch?"

"No, Flory, I couldn't eat a bite," said Meghan, and she couldn't wait for Jon to come in either. "I think I'll go have a look in the barn."

"Oh, Miss Meghan, you're soaked to the skin already," said Flory.

"But, Flory, I'm afraid something may have happened to him—I have to find him," said Meghan desperately, starting toward the door.

Before she reached it, she was stopped by a knock. It flashed through her head it could be someone with news of Jon and she rushed to answer, but it was only Harley. She saw that he had parked his car at the steps and it was loaded with his belongings.

Suddenly she didn't want him to go. He was someone sturdy and reliable to have around. But there, she mustn't start thinking like that again.

"I forgot to give Jon the keys to the cottage," he said, dangling them before her.

Meghan took them and slipped them in her pocket mechanically. Nothing mattered but Jon's whereabouts, his safety.

"Harley, I don't know what to think—Jon still hasn't come in," she said.

"Well, I wouldn't worry about it," said Harley. "As you said, he probably has some perfectly logical explanation."

"I was just about to run out to the barn and see if he's there—maybe waiting for the rain to slack," she said, knowing all the time rain never stopped Jon.

"Then perhaps you should just wait until he comes in," suggested Harley.

She shook her head, slinging her wet hair across her face. "No, I can't stand waiting—I have to find him."

She was conscious of becoming shrill, a bit hysterical.

Harley looked at her worriedly and offered, "I'll go with you."

"You don't have to," she said.

"But I think I'd better," he said.

As they left the kitchen, Meghan could not help being glad Harley was going with her. She might need his help.

Then again she was back out in the driving rain, half running, her feet slipping on the flooded ground. As they passed the toolshed, she saw Terrence tinkering with a piece of farm equipment.

He looked up to inquire, "Jon hasn't got back yet?"

"Not yet," said Meghan despairingly, not stopping.

"Maybe he's up to his old tricks," Terrence called after them.

Furious with him, Meghan made no answer and tore on through the steady, unrelenting rain, Harley at her side.

"Meghan, I hate to see you getting thin and pale again, worrying about him," Harley said, his wet, concerned face turned toward her.

"Please, Harley, don't act as if it's starting all over again," she cried, but that fear was deep inside her, no matter how much she fought against it or tried to deny it—the fear

Jon would start drinking again.

In a way it was more profoundly frightening than the threats she had received. "I couldn't bear it. I couldn't go through that again."

Pure hell it had been.

"I hope you don't have to," said Harley.

They flew past the scattering of outbuildings and the lake house. Skimmingly through the rain, Meghan saw the lake and could have sobbed at the happy times it brought to mind. They started up the slippery slope and more than once she would have fallen if Harley hadn't steadied her. He was good at that.

But she couldn't think about Harley—only Jon. He filled her very existence. And she had to get to him—before it was too late. That phrase began to hammer in her head: before it was too late.

Reaching the wide, shadowy doorway of the barn, they rushed in and were swallowed up in the dim expanse of it. Around Meghan swam the damp, moldy odor of hay, feed, and such.

Remembering Flory's warning about bats being in the loft, Meghan could not resist glancing up warily, but thank heaven she could not see any. If she had, in her overwrought state, she might have screamed and died on the spot. All she needed was one of those creatures to fly in her hair.

Because she was looking up and because of the semidarkness of the barn, she did not see Jon as quickly as Harley. She felt his hand tightening on her arm and heard him say,

"Well, we should have known."

Then she saw Jon—she was almost standing over him, and there was no way she could avoid him. He was sprawled grotesquely over some bags of feed, reeking of whiskey, an empty bottle beside him.

Flung back into the old nightmare time, Meghan stared down at him. His finely drawn, scarred face had the unknowing, uncaring look she knew so well. It was that of Jon sleeping one off. Dead to the world, dead to her, dead to himself.

As everything bright and hopeful slipped from her, Meghan recoiled in anguish from the figure at her feet. Unable to look at him, see him this way, she turned to the strong, upright man beside her.

"Take me away—I have to get away," she said, her face chalky white, her eyes dark and enormous with pain.

Harley put his arm around her and they fled the barn but not the heart-crushing scene there. That she took with her. Meghan would carry that with her vividly, tormentingly, the rest of her life.

Blindly, with Harley supporting her, she made it back through the cold, unceasing rain to the house. Leaving Harley to explain to Flory, she went upstairs, changed into dry clothes, caught up her purse and Dido. She would have to send for her other things—she had to get out of here immediately.

With no backward look, Meghan left her

room and was hurrying for the stairs when Stephanie called to her.

"Meghan, Meghan, what's up? Where are you going?" she asked, catching up with her.

"Back to Memphis," said Meghan, not stopping, her face set.

"Why? Where's Jon?" asked Stephanie, plucking at Meghan's sleeve, avid with curiosity.

"In the barn—drunk."

Stephanie drew in her breath and gazed at Meghan accusingly. Then she announced almost triumphantly, "I'm going to him—he needs me."

Then she went racing down the stairs. In a dull, deadlike way, Meghan followed more slowly and watched her snatch a coat from the hall tree and dash out the back door. People were always running about crazily because of Jon. But he didn't need poor, pretty Stephanie. He didn't need anyone—only the blasted bottle. She couldn't help him, Stephanie couldn't help him, no one could help him except Jon himself, and he seemed bent on destroying himself. She could not stay and see that happen.

Harley waited for her in the kitchen. He was always waiting for her—as Meghan was always waiting for Jon. But not anymore, not anymore.

She became conscious of Flory, distressed and troubled, coming to her and putting her arms around her.

"Oh, Miss Meghan, you think you should be leaving?" she asked.

"Yes, I'm not doing any good here, Flory. It's for the best." The best? No, what she had to look forward to was an empty life, an empty heart.

"But, Miss Meghan, this is only the first time he's back-slipped in a long time," Flory pointed out.

Meghan shook her head tiredly. "Oh, Flory, once he starts, there's no stopping him. He'll just go on and on."

"But, Miss Meghan, sometimes things are not what they seem," said Flory rather oddly. She looked as if she might be trying to tell Meghan something with her strange, inward-turned eyes.

"Oh, Flory, I saw him!" said Meghan. "Good-bye."

Meghan turned abruptly and left the cook staring after her in that peculiar, anxious way of hers. No need trying to figure Flory out.

And, going down the back steps to Harley's car, she silently said goodbye to the dark, melancholy house, to Jon. If only she could say goodbye to agony such as this.

CHAPTER SIXTEEN

Meghan cried inconsolably most of the way back to Memphis and was only vaguely aware of the rain-veiled countryside swimming by. She wanted the slick broad highway to carry her away from Blackthorn and the heartbreak she had experienced there, but at the same time leaving, tearing herself away was such a wrench.

Although it had been brief, she had known rapture there—with Jon. And as the miles flowed behind her, and she got farther and farther away from him, the stronger, sweeter image of him began to prevail in her mind, to outshine the crumpled, weak figure in the barn.

She saw him as she had that Monday on her return to Blackthorn. In that first ecstatic glimpse she had seen the Jon she had often hoped and prayed for.

Then in the library he had lowered his

flawed, firelit face to kiss her, but she had held back.

"You do still love me, don't you?" he had asked.

"I still love you, but—"

It had been enough for him that she still loved him, and his lips had come crashing down on hers. But loving in that sick, blind way was not enough. There had to be stability, respect, and a strong feeling of trust.

But, Jon, oh, Jon, it's killing me, tearing me right down the middle to leave you! All the joy of living goes with you. The years ahead seem so flat and empty without you.

Hearing her sob in her lonely corner of the seat, Harley reached over and pressed her cold, lifeless hand. And it passed through her hurting, throbbing head that his touch did not in any way thrill or excite her. Jon could thrill her with one dark, glowing glance, one softly spoken word. Yet Harley's presence was so warm and comforting, so soothing.

"I don't understand," she mumbled achingly, bewilderedly. "Jon seemed so happy. Why—why did he have to deliberately throw it all away, ruin everything?"

"Beats me," said Harley, shaking his head. "Maybe the guy just didn't know how lucky he was. But, Meghan, I don't think it would have ever worked. He's weak—he would always go back to drinking, disappointing you over and over again. And, heaven knows, it's been like this ever since his father's death. Sometimes I wonder about that."

She turned to him slowly, searching his bland, nondescript face in the fading afternoon light. "Harley! What're you saying? You're not suggesting his father's death was not an accident? That Jon—?"

She could not even put it into words.

"No, but you know how they never got along," said Harley, looking straight ahead, not for a second taking his eyes off the rain-slick road. "And if he did have something to do with it—mind you I'm not saying he did. But if he did, it could explain the drinking. He could be drowning out—"

Meghan could listen to no more and snapped, "Harley, you really don't know Jon at all if you think he could have possibly had anything to do with his father's death! He's not at all the violent type. He's just the opposite, very gentle. The only person he has ever turned against is himself. I know he and his father didn't get along. And Jon has always regretted not living up to his expectations, but for you to insinuate—"

At her raised voice, Dido, trying to sleep on her lap, looked up inquiringly.

"I'm sorry, I'm sorry," Harley hastened to apologize, backing off in the face of her anger. "I was only trying to figure out why he does it—why when he seems to have everything, he has to rely on alcohol."

"Well, I don't think anyone really knows why people drink," she said. "All I know is that it's a disease, and I was hoping Jon had it under control."

"Evidently he hadn't," said Harley, not gloatingly but merely as one stating a fact. "But, please, Meghan, let's not quarrel over Jon—let's not even talk about him. I'm only thinking of you and what he's done to you, how he's hurt you."

"Oh, I'll be all right," she said, finding a tissue in her purse and wiping her wet, aching face. "What I have to do now is to try to forget all about this and concentrate on my work—the shop—and try to make some sort of life for myself."

Women were always saying things like that, but was it ever enough? Could a career take the place of marriage, home, and family? She did not think so, but she would have to "make do," as Aunt Duffy used to say.

"I wish you would consider sharing a life with me," said Harley in his calm, measured way.

"No, Harley," she said firmly. She had made that mistake before. "I'm much too broken up and confused to think about anything like that now."

But the main reason she could not consider marriage with him was, she was not in love with him. Not wildly, madly, desperately. She knew that for sure because she was still crazily in love with Jon and probably always would be. Nothing could change that. He was there in her heart to stay, no matter what he did.

"Then can we be friends?" asked Harley.

She could not deny him that. "Yes, if you'll realize that's all we can ever be. But really I think you should be out trying to find someone else."

As soon as she said it, she knew it was a foolish thing to say. What if someone advised her to go out and find someone else when she was still aching and crying for Jon?

"But I don't want anyone else," he said in the stubborn, unyielding way that reminded Meghan of herself. "Don't you know how long I've loved you, Meghan? I used to watch you and Jon together, paddling across the lake or going off to gather wildflowers. And everything inside me wanted to be in his place, at your side, holding your hand. But instead there was always some chore for me to do, something Mr. Deverell wanted me to do, something Jon should have been doing."

She caught the resentment in his voice and looked at him in surprise. She hadn't known Harley Felton had such strong feelings in him. But maybe she didn't really know Harley. She had always been so full of Jon. She had thought—when she thought seriously about Harley at all—that he was easygoing and mainly interested in doing a good job at Blackthorn. Instead, he had secretly, smolderingly, envied Jon's leisurely lifestyle, envied Jon because she loved him.

"Harley, you can be proud of the job you did at Blackthorn and how you conducted yourself there. You don't know how much the family depended on you. And now that you'll be getting a place of your own, I know you'll prosper and do well there, too."

It was a pat little speech, but it was the best she could do—crushed and wounded as she was. Still, she meant it. She wanted the best for Harley.

"The only thing, I'll be real lonely," he said with a deep sigh.

Meghan would be lonely, too. How different things would have been if today hadn't happened, if she and Jon could have carried out their plans. She could have helped him around the plantation, and they had talked of having children . . .

But there now, she had to stop thinking about all that. She had to let go of those too-wonderful, too-good-to-be-true dreams. She mustn't lose herself in despair.

It was late afternoon and still raining when they reached Memphis. As cities went, she supposed it was all right, but today the traffic-jammed streets and crowded buildings only added to her unhappiness. She wanted the quiet and sweep of Blackthorn. But really there was no peace and joy there, not with Jon drinking again.

Silently, wrapped in his own thoughts, Harley worked his careful way through the maze of streets to her deserted little house. The shadowy outline of it further depressed her. Meghan hated coming back to this solitary, loveless existence. She wanted Jon—oh, how she wanted Jon and his arms holding her close. Was it only this morning he had kissed her and promised to be back in time for lunch? So many times he had promised and broken his promise.

As Harley pulled in the drive, she asked, "Would you like to come in? I think I could find enough food in the fridge to make us some sort of supper."

It was the least she could do for him after all he had done for her—driven her home and tried to comfort her. Besides, she didn't want to go in that dark, empty house by herself. After all, it was there she had received the threatening call and found the skull-and-crossbones drawing on her door. She had the uneasy feeling all that wasn't finished yet.

"If it's not too much trouble," said Harley.

She gathered up Dido and her handbag and stepped out into the streaming weather and twilight. What a time to be coming home.

They made a dash for it and, as they ran up onto the porch, she heard the phone shrilling through the forlorn little house. Like that other time, she thought tiredly, when she had got the threatening call. Fumbling for her key, she hoped it wasn't another one of those. But if it was, at least she wouldn't be alone this time.

CHAPTER SEVENTEEN

Meghan managed to get the door open and ran in ahead of Harley to the phone in her bedroom. It could be the anonymous caller. Then again, it could be...Jon. He could be calling to beg her forgiveness. He was usually very contrite after one of his binges. Her hand was shaking and her heart pounding as she picked up the phone.

"Hello," she said hesitantly and held her breath.

"Miss Meghan—"

"Flory!" She certainly hadn't expected her. "Is that you? Is anything wrong?"

"Well, no more than usual," said the quavering, uncertain voice. "But, Miss Meghan, I was just worried about you, wondering if you'd got there safely in the rain and all."

"I'm fine, Flory." Not really. She was miserable, actually. Then she had to ask, "Everyone there all right?"

Everyone was another name for Jon.

Flory knew who she meant. "Mr. Jon's still groggy and not making much sense."

"I can imagine," said Meghan with irony.

"Miss Stephanie and Mr. Terrence took him up and put him to bed," said Flory. "He'll be all right when he . . . comes out of it. But I've been more concerned about you, Miss Meghan. I've just had this feeling—I don't know how to explain it—that you're in some kind of deep trouble."

"Well, that's probably because of the threatening calls," said Meghan as calmly as she could, even trying for a yawn. All the same, she knew Flory's premonitions were not to be sneezed at, or yawned at.

Muddled as she was, Flory had proved more than once to have some kind of second sight. However, Meghan could not see that she was in any deep trouble at the moment, unless one counted having a broken heart deep trouble.

She tried to reassure Flory. "Really, we arrived safely, and Harley's here with me and everything's fine. So not to worry."

"You say Mr. Harley's there with you?"

"Yes, I thought I would whip up a bit of supper for him since he was good enough to bring me in," said Meghan.

"Well, be careful, Miss Meghan," said Flory, not sounding too reassured. "Maybe it was foolish of me to worry, but I couldn't rest until I called you."

"I'm fine," said Meghan again. "Bye-bye now."

"Goodbye, Miss Meghan." She sounded reluctant to hang up, as if she had more to say but wasn't sure she should say it, or how to say it.

Meghan eased the receiver down, not wanting to break the connection either. She did not know why, but it seemed like a safety line tying her to Blackthorn. She had no idea why Blackthorn seemed like a haven. After all, the mourning-veil incident had happened there.

But what about Flory's call? The poor woman must have been anxious indeed to have called—she hadn't called Meghan before. What if she were merely trying to find out if Meghan was alone? Then later tonight she could hop in that old Chevy of hers, drive into Memphis, and...

No, no, she simply couldn't think that about Flory! Flory had seemed genuinely concerned about her. And Meghan felt uneasy because Flory felt uneasy about her. If Flory really did have second sight or E.S.P. or whatever...

As Meghan stood staring down at the phone, something caused her to turn, and she jumped seeing the bulky, shadowy figure in the doorway. But it was only Harley. Her nerves must really be bad for her to jump at the sight of Harley.

"Are you all right?" he asked, seeing her starkly white face in the gloom of the room. She hadn't turned on the light and the only illumination slanting in was from the living room, and he blocked out most of that.

"Yes, I was afraid it might be another of

those calls, but it was only Flory wanting to know if I had got here safely," she said, trying to shrug off her tenseness as she walked toward him.

"Another of those calls?" he repeated, looking puzzled. "Meghan, have you been receiving annoying phone calls?"

"Annoying and threatening. Haven't I told you?" she asked, surprised she hadn't.

So while she was opening a can of oyster stew and throwing together something of a meal, she told him about the calls—the one she had received and the one Flory had received. "Oh, yes, and there was an awful drawing."

"Drawing?" he said, looking more and more perturbed.

"It was of a skull and crossbones and tacked to my door," she told him as she put bread and cheese in the oven. Grilled-cheese sandwiches and the stew would have to do. And coffee—decaf, by all means.

"And you never told me," said Harley, standing around, mostly in the way, not helping as Jon would have done. But she must not think about Jon.

"Meghan, I wish you would let me know when things like that happen," said Harley scoldingly.

"I didn't think—so much has been going on," she said, getting out bowls.

"Well, listen, I'll be staying in a hotel tonight and, as soon as I check in, I'll call and

let you know where I am so you can reach
me—should you need me. And I want you to
promise to call me if anything else happens."

She promised she would and they sat down
to steaming bowls of oyster stew and grilled-
cheese sandwiches. She could not help thinking how different this was from the supper she
had prepared for Jon. Although she had been
upset then by the calls and the drawing, the
candlelit dinner had a romance and glamour
to it. He had brought flowers and his eyes had
glowed across the table.

As she thought of that, she happened to
glance at Harley, and there was a knowing,
disapproving look in his squarish face, as if
he knew she was thinking about Jon.

"Meghan, believe me, it wouldn't have
worked," he said. "You're young and have your
life before you. You don't have to go on and
on letting that guy ruin it for you."

She put down her spoon, wondering why she
had thought oyster stew such a good idea. She
looked up with large, misty eyes. "But, Harley,
he and I could have been so happy. We were
happy these past few days—and I can't understand why he would suddenly—and for no
reason—go back to drinking. I know this may
sound crazy, but it seems so out of character."

"Out of character?" he said incredulously.
"It seems perfectly in character to me—the
old Jon acting true to form."

"But that's just it—he's been like a new Jon,
responsible and mature. He hadn't had a drink

in two years, and then for him—"

"It could be that the thought of marriage and the responsibility of it was too much for him," suggested Harley. With a shrug, he changed the subject. "Say, this stew is really good—hits the spot."

She reached for a sandwich and tried to eat but was only halfhearted about it. She kept thinking about her own words: "out of character." That scene in the barn was totally out of character with the new strong Jon. It was almost as if—as if it had been arranged, staged. What if—?

Her thoughts broke off and she gave a little leap as the phone rang.

"Want me to get it?" asked Harley, half rising.

"No, I'll take it," she said. "If it is the anonymous caller, I may be able to tell who it is."

And if it's Jon, she thought as she left the table, I'll tell him not to call anymore, that it's all over for us. Going into the bedroom, Meghan closed the door, wanting this conversation to be private.

"Meg?" It was Jon, and in spite of everything, a thrill shot through her at the sound of his voice.

"Jon, really, I don't think we have anything to say to each other—ever," she said, starting to hang up, not wanting to give that charm of his a chance to overcome her better judgment.

"No, Meg!" He sounded really desperate. "I haven't been drinking."

"Oh, Jon, I saw you with my own eyes," she said disgustedly. What kind of fool did he take her for?

"You saw what you were meant to see," he said. "Meg, I swear I haven't touched a drop— except for that which was poured all over me."

"Poured all over you?" she said incredulously. Was it—could it be possible—?

"The last thing I remember was going over some papers with Harley, and he asked me if I would like a cup of coffee. Like a fool I said yes. Meg, he put something in that coffee."

She stood deadly still, totally silent, letting the pieces of what he was saying fall into place and, although it came out a frightening, terrifying picture, it made more sense than that tableau in the barn.

"Meg?" he said. "Are you still there?"

"Yes," she managed, her throat very dry.

"Harley's not there, is he?" he asked anxiously.

"In the other room," she said, swallowing hard.

"Oh, my heaven," he groaned. Then, as if thinking fast, he said, "Try to get rid of him. If you can't, be very careful—until I can get there. Oh, and, Meg, it might be best if you don't let on that you know. The man's desperate and could try anything. I don't mean to alarm you, but when I was in the cottage, I saw a gun on his mantel. He said it was for protection, but you can't tell. I think he's really deranged. As far as I'm concerned, he's already proved he can be dangerous."

CHAPTER EIGHTEEN

Before hanging up, Meghan asked quickly, "Jon, do you think you should drive after being drugged?"

"I'll have Terrence drive me in—it may take the two of us to deal with Harley, anyway," he said. "But don't you worry about me. You just watch out for yourself."

"Jon," she said before he could break the connection, "I'm sorry I—"

"We'll talk about that later." He seemed anxious to be on his way to her.

"I love you," she said.

"Love you, too. Take care."

And that was all. Meghan hadn't even his voice to sustain her. She was left alone in her bedroom, severed from him with a warped, twisted man in the next room.

Dangerous, Jon had said, and perhaps he was. Anyone who would put a knockout pill in someone's coffee and arrange that scene in the barn had to be more than a little unstable.

Harley had deceived her, too, not only today but those two years he had courted her and not told her Jon had quit drinking. He was indeed not to be trusted.

Oh, and the threatening calls and the skull-and-crossbones drawing and the veil around Dido's neck—he must have done those things, too, because she had gone back to Jon. And because he was—beneath that calm, composed, friendly exterior—a spiteful, vengeful man. There was no telling what he might do when he realized he had been found out. Something desperate, no doubt.

But she couldn't hang about in here. She must go to Harley and not let on, play it cool. She had to keep him steady and in control somehow until Jon and Terrence got there. It was such a long way from Blackthorn, though. They were probably only now barreling down the drive, and it was such a bad night, they would not be able to make good time.

Please, she prayed, don't let them be reckless. Let them get here safely.

Now to go in there to that madman. She mustn't let Harley see she was afraid. How could she do that when she was shaking all over?

"Meghan, are you all right in there?" he called, sounding as if he were standing right against the door. She hoped he hadn't been standing there all the time, listening to her conversation with Jon.

"Yes, be right out," she said, willing herself not to tremble. Then rigidly she opened the door and faced him, smiling. "That Mrs. Macklin—she can really talk a leg off you."

"Mrs. Macklin?" he asked, watching her closely, faint suspicion showing in his face. He must know Jon would call as soon as he came out of it.

"My neighbor. She saw your car out front and wanted to be sure it was yours and someone wasn't trying to break in. I think, too, she was curious about me coming back. But I assured her everything was all right." Meghan sat down opposite him at the table and picked up the partly eaten sandwich. If only she could swallow without choking. "Oh, can I make you another sandwich, warm your coffee?"

"No, thanks." He was still watching her, his eyes slightly narrowed. "But are you sure you're O.K.? You're looking a little pale—and your hand's trembling."

"Well, it's been quite a day," she said with a shaky sigh. And it wasn't over yet.

"It kills me to see what Jon does to you—tears you apart like this," he said.

"All that's over now," she said and found herself wondering about that mark on his face. She had thought he had nicked himself shaving, but it wasn't a razor nick—it was an animal's scratch. Had he got that when he tied the veil around Dido's neck?

"I wish we could go away somewhere and start all over," Harley was saying. "You and I."

She shook her head and said gently, "No, it's best I stay here and try to work things out for myself."

"Whatever you do—don't let Jon talk you into going back to him," he said, his face hard, his eyes stony.

"Oh, I won't," she said emphatically. "Today finished it for me."

"He'll probably come to you with some excuse, but don't you believe him. He can only mean misery for you."

"I suppose you're right," she said, sighing.

Somehow she got the sandwich down and was drinking the last of her tepid coffee when the phone rang.

"Now who can that be?" she said, getting up.

"Let me get it this time," he said. "If it's that anonymous caller—or Jon—I don't want you bothered. I'll deal with whoever it is."

She did not try to stop him as he strode across the room, looking like the strong, sensible type who could handle anything. She prayed it wasn't someone from Blackthorn saying Jon was on the way. She doubted Jon would call again. He was probably wasting no time getting to her. It could be one of her customers wanting to know if she had a crystal butter dish or something.

Mechanically Meghan began clearing off the table. She was stacking the dishes in the sink when Harley returned. She could tell at once by his expression that he was incensed, so much so he could not speak for a moment. He could only glare at her.

"Who was it?" she asked, trying to sound casual. Who could have called to anger him like that?

"Mrs. Macklin," he said. "She was checking to make sure that was my car out front and that you were O.K. What I'd like to know is—who called a while ago?"

Meghan shrieked to herself and could only stand there, staring at him, trapped in her own lie, not knowing how to get out of it, what to say.

"It was Jon, wasn't it?" he asked, moving closer, his eyes boring into hers. "Don't lie to me, Meghan. It was Jon who called before, wasn't it?"

Seeing no way out of it, she nodded. "Yes, Harley, it was Jon."

"And what did he say?"

"Oh, he had some wild story about your putting a knockout pill in his coffee," she said, shrugging.

He smiled contemptuously, his eyes remaining hard as rock. "Leave it to Jon to think of something like that—put the blame on me. But why didn't you tell me before?"

"I—I didn't think it really worth repeating, and I didn't want to upset you," she said. Indeed, she hadn't wanted to upset him.

"So you made up that story about Mrs. Macklin," he said disapprovingly, "I never knew you could be so devious. It's not like you.

I want you never, never to lie to me again—
I want you always, always to be honest with
me."

"I'm sorry," she said. She was sorry only that
she hadn't got away with it.

"What else did he say?" Harley asked,
searching her face penetratingly.

"Not much—he sounded a little as if he were
still...under the influence," she said. That
wasn't too much of a fib. Jon had sounded as
though the drug hadn't quite worn off, that
he was struggling to clear his head.

"Probably had a drink or two more," Harley
surmised. "You know, Meghan, the more I
think about it, the more I think it could've
been Jon making those threatening calls and
doing all that other crazy stuff."

"Oh, Harley, I don't know about that."

"Because of you and me—our friendship—
because you were considering marrying me,"
he said.

"Do you really think so?" she said, as if reluctantly pondering the possibility. Never in
her life had she done so much acting.

"He may have even been drinking then—
when he made those calls," he continued. "You
know, I never did believe he had really given
up booze."

"Apparently, he hasn't," she said and turned
to start on the dishes. "But, please, Harley,
let's not talk about Jon anymore."

"Gladly. I can't say I care for the subject,"
he said with a grimace. And yet—he couldn't

or wouldn't let the subject alone. "Just one more thing before we drop it. He didn't say anything about trying to see you again?"

She shook her head, avoiding his hard, probing eyes. "No, I told him it was no use—that it was over, that we're through."

"Good girl," Harley said, patting her on the shoulder. "It's for the best, you know, and you'll soon get over him."

"I hope so," Meghan said, and that was the biggest lie of all. She had loved Jon for years and would go on loving him.

"In time you and I may get back together as we were before you went back to Blackthorn," Harley said.

"Oh, Harley, I don't think—" she said falteringly. No need letting him build up his hopes on that score again. "Anyway, I'm much too tired and confused to think about anything like that now."

"I just want you to know I'll be there waiting for you," he said.

"It's good to know I have a friend like you," she said. With a little more practice, she could become quite an expert liar. But she wasn't sure he believed her altogether. He had a watchful, wary look about him. The Mrs. Macklin thing had shaken his trust in her.

"We can't ever let anyone come between us again," he said.

"I always know I can count on you, Harley," Meghan said. That was how she had felt about him in the past—that he was solid and dependable and good. She hadn't known the real Harley Felton.

"One thing for sure, you could never count on Jon Deverell," he said bitterly. "You'd never know from one day till the next—"

He was interrupted by a pounding on the door, and they turned to stare at each other.

"Now, who the devil can that be?" he asked, scowling.

"I have no idea," she said, drying her hands.

It was true. She had no idea who was banging on the door. Jon and Terrence hadn't had time to get in from Blackthorn. But whoever it was, she was thankful for him/her and started toward the door. Now she wouldn't be alone with this madman.

"I had better go with you," said Harley, right at her elbow.

Passing through the living quarters to the shop, she looked out the display window and gasped, "The police!"

CHAPTER NINETEEN

Harley, looking over Meghan's shoulder, swore under his breath. "You called them, didn't you—after you talked to Jon?"

"No, I didn't," she said. But it wasn't a bad idea. Those two robust uniformed men out there gave her an immense feeling of security. "Shouldn't we see what they want?"

He hesitated, as if planning some sort of strategy.

"All right, open up, tell them everything's fine, and I'll back you up."

She saw his hand go to his pocket and her eyes widened. He had a gun. One word to the police about him, and she was dead.

He nudged her toward the door and somehow she unbolted it, got it open. Then she was facing the policemen on the rain-swept porch. In her excitement, all she noticed about the pair was that one was white and one was black. Angels from heaven, no less.

"What is it, Officers?" asked Harley, standing directly behind her, so close that she felt his breath against her cheek. She also felt the gun.

"We've had a call that there might be trouble here," said the black policeman, giving Harley a sharp, keen-eyed look.

"There's no trouble here," said Harley, as if surprised. "We're just two old friends spending a quiet evening together."

How convincing he could sound, thought Meghan, so sane. That one hand resting on her shoulder was a masterly touch.

"Are you all right, miss?" asked the other officer.

She nodded. "Yes, I'm fine."

"What's this all about?" asked Harley, giving the impression of one totally in the dark. "Has someone seen prowlers—or something?"

"No, we were merely asked to check this residence."

And evidently that was all the policemen meant to tell them. Perhaps it was all they knew. If Jon had called them, he would not have had time to tell them the whole story. He, with Terrence, was probably even now barreling down the highway to Memphis.

"I think I can explain," said Harley. "Miss Latimer's ex-fiance is very jealous of my seeing her. He probably called—he drinks heavily and is not very reliable."

The officers made no response to this, and one said, "We'll be in the vicinity if you need us."

"I doubt we shall unless Jon—Mr. Deverell—comes and starts trouble," said Harley.

In dismay, Meghan watched the policemen return to the patrol car. Oh, no, they were leaving her to this lunatic. How were they to know he had a gun? All they had was a report from some frantic young man that his fiance could be in danger. They had done their duty, checked her residence, and found her unharmed with a seemingly calm, stable man. No crime had been committed.

With a sinking heart, Meghan saw the patrol car roll away—and with rising panic she saw Harley lock the door. She wondered wildly if he meant to hold her hostage. What was going on in that crazy, mixed-up head?

"Harley, it's been a long day," she said.

He shook his head obdurately. "I'm not going, Meghan, and you're not going. We're going to stay here and spend our last hours together."

"Last hours?" she repeated, alarmed.

He took her arm and drew her back into the living quarters.

"Now let's sit down and talk about this quietly. You and Jon are always so emotional about everything."

He pushed her roughly onto the sofa and sat down beside her, taking her hand in his. "Now we're all comfy cozy."

Far from comfy or cozy, she asked, "Harley, what did you mean by our last hours?"

"Precisely what you think I meant," he said, smiling. "You and I are going to have some time together. Don't you think you owe me at least one night after all I've done and suffered for you?"

"I'm grateful, yes, but—"

"Then give me a little time, that's all I ask," he said, letting go of her hand to put his arm around her and draw her over to him.

"Harley, please," she said, trying to pull away from him but not succeeding. He was strong, very strong. "You—you can't get away with this. The police are cruising around out there, and Jon's on his way."

"Just let any of them try to break in," he said. "I've thought about killing Jon for a long time, anyway—and I almost did once or twice. But too many accidents at Blackthorn would have looked suspicious."

"Accidents?" she repeated, staring at him with the dawning of new revelation. "You mean Mr. Deverell's death wasn't an accident?"

"In a way it was an accident. You see, I heard the old man tell Jon to clean the guns, but Jon went trotting off with you to pick daisies or something, and Mr. Deverell decided to do the job himself, not knowing one of the guns was loaded. So he got the bullet meant for Jon. Oh, well." Harley shrugged. "Not much loss either way. Old Deverell was an arrogant devil and drove me as if I were a slave. And then I tried to fix Jon's car—but he just hit the gate—and no one was hurt."

"Harley, Harley," she said, trying to call back the Harley she had known—or thought she had known. But he seemed quite beyond recall. There was nothing in the face of this cold, unfeeling stranger that was like that old Harley. But then that Harley had never really existed. Inside, he had been like this for years—a smoldering, scheming murderer.

"But let's not think about anything but us, Meg. Let's take these few hours we have left and make the most of them." He pulled her closer to him and lowered his face to hers.

She turned away before he could kiss her. Talking. She had to keep him talking.

"You keep saying things like last hours, few hours—Harley, you're not really thinking of—?"

"Oh, Meghan, what have either of us to live for—you would have only a life of hell with Jon, and my life would be meaningless without you, so I'll just save us both from that."

"You mean—?" She swallowed painfully. "You mean to—shoot us both?"

But, of course, that was what he meant.

"Yes, but you needn't look so scared. It will be over before you know it. Then we can both rest in peace, side by side," he said, as if he were looking forward to it.

"But, Harley, I don't want to die. I'm not ready to die." She wanted desperately to live, to live that life she and Jon had spoken of.

"You have no choice, my dear Meghan. You deserve to die. You've used me, encouraged me. Then you went running back to Jon without a backward glance at me. But tonight's not going to be that way. Tonight's mine."

He caught her closer so that she thought he would crack her ribs. She tried to struggle to get away from him, but he held fast and, bending his head, pressed his lips to hers. It was no kiss of love or tenderness—only an act of vindicative force, a show of power.

"Please, Harley," she said faintly. "Don't—"

"Why not? You let Jon kiss you—plenty of times. I've seen you. Now it's my turn."

He leaned over to kiss her again when mercifully there was a hammering on the door.

"Let's hope it's Jon," he said, getting up, his hand going to his pocket.

"No, Harley, no," she cried, trying to hold him.

But he broke away and headed for the door.

She ran after him, praying wildly, "Please, don't let it be Jon."

In the shop they both looked out the display window, and Meghan saw in a rush of relief the short, stocky figure of Mrs. Macklin and her beast of a dog. Lorenzo was almost as big as Mrs. Macklin herself.

"It's only Mrs. Macklin from next door," she said.

"Tell her to go away—tell her everything's all right," Harley ordered.

"No, she'll be suspicious. She's very suspicious, anyway. She'll know something's wrong if I don't talk to her. She'll get the police back here."

"All right, but make it quick," he said. "And, Meghan, don't try anything."

She went to the door and opened it.

"Why, Mrs. Macklin," she said.

"I saw the police here and I had to come over to see if everything's all right," said the dear, nosy woman.

"Oh, yes, everything's fine," said Meghan.

"Are you sure?" asked Mrs. Macklin, peering at her. "You don't look so good."

"I'm all right," said Meghan, even as she wavered on the verge of a nervous collapse. "Harley's here with me."

No doubt Mrs. Macklin thought that strange, too. She knew Meghan had planned to go back to Jon. So what was she doing here with another man and looking scared to death? Something in all this wasn't right and the woman wasn't budging until she found out what was going on.

"Then why were the police here?" she wanted to know.

Harley stepped out of the shadows of the shop then, and the dog gave a low growl.

"Good evening, Mrs. Macklin," he said calmly. "We appreciate your concern but, as you can see, everything's O.K. here."

"The police?"

"We suspect Jon Deverell called them—he's drinking and raving because Meghan has left him again," explained Harley, making it all sound plausible, more so than the truth.

Mrs. Macklin did not seem quite satisfied.

"Do you think Mr. Deverell will be coming in?"

"He may," said Harley. "But we think we can handle him, and the police have been notified."

"I hope there's no trouble," said Mrs. Macklin.

"Good night, Mrs. Macklin," said Harley, and before she could say more, he closed the door.

CHAPTER TWENTY

With the locking of the shop door, Meghan knew with a cold finality everyone was being shut out. It was now entirely up to her to get out of this living nightmare. No one from the outside could rescue her—not Mrs. Macklin, not Jon or the police. She had to save not only herself but Jon as well because, when he drove up, Harley would be waiting for him.

But what could she do against this crazed man with a gun? He was bigger and stronger than she. She could not wrest that deadly weapon from him.

About all she could do at the moment was talk and try to divert him until she could think of something.

"You know, Harley, you really aroused Mrs. Macklin's suspicions by slamming the door in her face that way," she said while her brain churned with ways to escape. Maybe she could make up some excuse to get into her bedroom and crawl out the window. No, he would never let her out of his sight that long.

Harley shrugged. "To hell with her. Old busybody—she can't do anything. No one can do anything. It's fated we have this one glorious night together. And if your precious Jon gets in the way, it's curtains for him, too. Now let's get back to where we were before we were interrupted."

He rubbed his strong countryman's hands together eagerly. Harley meant it was back to the sofa, and she could not endure the thought of him holding and kissing her again—not to mention ultimately killing her. There had to be some way out of this nightmare, there had to be. Think, Meghan, think.

As they were passing through the dimly lit shop, her hand brushed against an old flatiron on one of the display tables. Instinctively, furtively, her fingers curled around the cold iron handle. If she could hurl it at him...

He laughed behind her. "Don't try it, Meghan."

Reluctantly she let go of the iron and they passed on to the living quarters. When they were walking toward the sofa, he stopped suddenly.

"What was that?" he asked, instantly alert.

She listened. "Oh, it's only Dido scratching on the back door, wanting out. I always let her out at this time—I'd better let her go."

"Blasted cat," he said, stroking his chin

where Dido had scratched him. "All right, let her out."

Meghan hoped against hope Harley would not accompany her, but he did, evidently taking no chances. Crossing the kitchen, she unbolted the door and opened it. The cool, sweet air of freedom blew against her face, beckoning to her. It was now or never.

As Dido darted out, Meghan made as if to close the door. Instead, she reached for the light switch and threw the kitchen into total darkness. Harley, who was only a yard or two from her, lunged for her, but she slipped out of his grasp and plunged out into the rain and night.

Not bothering with the back steps, almost as one with wings, she jumped down all three and tore across the backyard. He came after her but, not knowing the territory as well as she, stumbled over the garbage can.

That gave Meghan time to turn the corner of the house and make for the gate.

As she was unlatching it, she heard him splashing through the grass after her and shouting wildly, "Stop or I'll shoot!"

Instead, she tore the gate open and went racing across Mrs. Macklin's scrap of a lawn. Harley fired at her and she screamed, but he missed.

"You can't get away with it," Harley yelled. "I'll get Jon for keeps. You know, I'm the one who started him drinking. I bought him booze at first, made him feel guilty. But he stopped drinking two years ago. Well, tonight I'll get him with a bullet!"

Not slowing down, she glanced over her shoulder and saw Harley was giving up for the moment and going back into the cottage—to wait for Jon. He would punish her, get even with her that way.

Flying up to Mrs. Macklin's porch, Meghan pounded on the door. Lorenzo began to bark from inside, and the old woman asked quaveringly, "Who is it?"

"Meghan Latimer. Please, let me in!"

She opened up enough to jerk Meghan inside. "Get in here, girl."

As Meghan stood panting and dripping, Mrs. Macklin slammed the door and locked it.

"Now, what's this all about?"

"Can't explain now," said Meghan breathlessly. "Call the police. Harley's insane, and he's got a gun."

"Gun!" Mrs. Macklin asked no more questions and hurried as fast as she could on her short legs to the phone. Meghan dragged along after her, not wanting to let her out of sight.

Mrs. Macklin did not even have to consult the police number pinned conspicuously over her phone. "This is Mrs. Macklin. Send somebody over here quick. There's bad trouble next door—man over there has gone berserk and he's got a gun." She forced them to believe her.

Then she gave them Meghan's house number and said emphatically, "Don't worry, we'll stay in."

She hung up and turned to Meghan, her face alive with the excitement of it all. "Police are on their way. Said we're to stay inside with the doors locked. But if that Harley fellow's as crazy as you say he is, he could come over and shoot the windows out and—"

Meghan shook her head. "No, I think now he's decided to wait and get Jon. He knows that would destroy me as certainly as anything. Oh, Mrs. Macklin, maybe I should have stayed and tried to prevent that!"

"No, you did right in getting away from him," said Mrs. Macklin. "What I've seen of young Deverell, he can take care of himself and, besides, the police will be here in a jiffy."

And they were. Within minutes, three squad cars, blue lights flashing, pulled up—two in front of Meghan's cottage and one in front of Mrs. Macklin's. The two officers Meghan had seen earlier dodged around trees and bushes and finally slipped up to Mrs. Macklin's porch.

Mrs. Macklin let them in and, through chattering teeth, Meghan told them of her wild, incredible evening. They eyed her admiringly when she related how she had escaped.

"But the last thing Harley said was he was going to get Jon," she told them. That icy fear was all she could think of now.

"Don't worry, miss, we've got the street blocked off—he can't come through," one of them assured her.

"Oh, thank God, thank God," she whispered gratefully.

But as the two policemen left to join the others surrounding the cottage, she could not help thinking how anxious Jon would be on arriving and finding himself unable to get to her. He wouldn't know what was going on, what was happening to her.

"I'll get my binoculars," Mrs. Macklin offered. "And maybe you can see if his car's down at the end of the street."

When Meghan peeked around a window shade and through the binoculars, she was unable to see anything except squad cars, darkness, and rain.

Would it ever stop raining? she wondered as she handed the binoculars back to Mrs. Macklin. Would this long nightmare ever be over?

Mrs. Macklin used the binoculars to tell Meghan what was going on next door. "They're closing in on him—oh, did you hear that?"

Meghan nodded silently and covered her ears, but no more shots sounded. Only that one.

"I can't tell if it came from inside or outside," said Mrs. Macklin.

"It came from inside," said Meghan, not seeing but knowing. Harley had shot himself—she was suddenly, positively sure of it. He would never let the police take him. If he could not take her and Jon with him, he would go by himself, escape in that way. "My life would be meaningless without you," he had said.

An officer came over to tell them that was indeed what had happened. Harley had been found on the sofa, shot through the head, the gun on the floor beside him.

As the policeman was leaving, Jon, ashen-faced and tight-lipped, burst in and Meghan rushed over to him. They held each other as if they would never let go. She would never, never leave him again. No matter what.

"Darling, darling, are you all right?" Jon asked anxiously, his whole face still dark with fear.

"I am now," she said, feasting her eyes on his dear, finely drawn features. Only a little while ago she had thought she would never see him again.

"He didn't—he didn't harm you?" Jon asked.

"No, but he tried," she said, snuggling even closer to Jon at the thought of her narrow escape. That mad dash through the rain would haunt her the rest of her life.

"Well, he can't hurt anyone ever again," Jon said, grimly relieved. "It's all over. Let's get out of here—let's go home."

Meghan turned and embraced Mrs. Macklin. "I don't know what to say—how to thank you."

"I'm just glad I was here and that you're safe," said Mrs. Macklin, patting her shoulder. "And I hope you and Mr. Deverell will be happy—and forget all about this."

As they stepped out, reporters and television cameras were waiting for them. Meghan ducked her head. What a sight she must be with her stringy hair and crumpled clothes. And she did not think she could go over the story again. Jon gallantly shielded her from the reporters.

"Miss Latimer has been through a very harrowing experience this evening and can't say anything now," he said, pushing through the gathering.

Still, questions were hurled at her as Jon and Meghan hurried to the car where Terrence waited for them with the motor going. Jon helped her in, and they took off after Dido jumped in, too.

Sitting between Jon and Terrence, Meghan suddenly began to cry.

"Sweetheart," said Jon tenderly, kissing her wet face. "Don't cry now—it's all over and we're going home."

There was magic to his words, but she wasn't entirely rejoicing.

"Oh, Jon, I'm so sorry I thought you—"

"Had gone off the wagon?"

She nodded miserably.

"But, honey, I don't blame you for that," he said understandingly. "I can see how you would think I was pie-eyed. Harley made it look good."

"Maniac," muttered Terrence.

"But I should have trusted you," she said. "I should have stuck by you."

"Yes, you should have," he said lightly. "But no one's perfect. I forgive you. Just see that it doesn't happen again. Now put that tired head on my shoulder. Forget about today and try to rest."

Meghan doubted she could ever rest again, but, with her head right where it belonged, she not only rested but drifted off to sleep. She was still sleeping when Jon carried her upstairs and covered her with a quilt.

When she awoke, the rain had finally stopped. The sun was coming up, and a bright new day was beginning.